Eva took a stead to the moment u **you."**

Nick lowered the ice pack. "It does?"

"I mean, I suppose a kiss is no big deal, but—"

"I disagree." Heat flickered in his eyes. "We're not kids playing games. I don't kiss a woman for the heck of it. Not these days."

Her breathing quickened. "Then we're on the same page."

His mouth curved in a soft smile. "Not yet. But we're reading the same book. That's a good start."

"We've established that we're not indiscriminate kissers."

"Right."

"I have a reason for not kissing you a while ago." She paused. "There's something you need to know."

His stance widened and his jaw tensed as he physically braced himself. "Okay."

TRUE-BLUE COWBOY

THE BUCKSKIN BROTHERHOOD

Vicki Lewis Thompson

Ocean Dance Press

TRUE-BLUE COWBOY
© 2020 Vicki Lewis Thompson

ISBN: 978-1-946759-89-4

Ocean Dance Press LLC
PO Box 69901
Oro Valley, AZ 85737

Cover art by Lee Hyat Designs

Visit the author's website at
VickiLewisThompson.com

1

Nick La Grande settled in the upholstered salon chair, propped his boots on the metal footrest and glanced in the mirror. Meeting the gaze of the smiling woman standing behind him filled his chest with warmth.

He didn't permit that warmth to travel south, though. Eva Kilpatrick had never shown the slightest interest in him, so he'd keep his reaction under control and his fantasies to himself.

She'd never know he'd pictured her lying beneath him, her green eyes smoldering with desire. Her hair, which she'd colored a rich peacock blue, would be even more amazing spread out on a snowy white pillow.

Maintaining eye contact in the mirror, she tunneled her fingers through his somewhat ordinary brown hair. "We need to make you look really hot for the bachelor auction."

"I like the sound of that." And he loved when she fooled with his hair.

"What do you think of adding some blond highlights?"

He tensed. "So I'll look like CJ?" He'd give his life for CJ Andrews. But Eva was *not* coloring his hair to match the golden locks of her former crush now that CJ was off the market.

She blinked. "You don't look anything like CJ."

So true, and unfortunately, that cowboy, a member of the Buckskin Brotherhood and one of Nick's closest friends, was her gold standard. He caught his own reflection in the mirror. Envy didn't look good on him. He flashed her a smile. "You're right. I'm prettier."

In the chair next to him, Rafe snorted. "And a huge pain in the patoot." He laid back for his shampoo and his horizontal six-six frame brought his boots within inches of a magazine rack on the far wall. "Can't believe I let you talk me into this auction thing."

"*Calme-toi*, Rafe." Josette rubbed shampoo into his hair. "Raptors Rise is a good cause."

"Yes, ma'am." He took a breath. "I'm happy to do my part."

Nick grinned. Nothing like a mild rebuke from a woman Rafe thought of as a beloved auntie to adjust his attitude.

"So." Eva rested her hands on Nick's shoulders, her gaze amused. "Blond highlights?"

She was a toucher. During appointments, she'd often stand this way, her hands on the client's shoulders, creating a temporary bond. She treated her customers as friends, and if that was all he ever became, he'd learn to live with it.

The lilt in her voice told him she'd enjoy coloring his hair. Because of that, he was tempted to agree. Maybe she wasn't trying to make him look like CJ. But, damn it, he'd wince every time he glanced in the mirror.

He maintained his smile. "I appreciate the suggestion, but it wouldn't work for me." Too bad if she preferred blond hair to brown. Dying his hair to spark her interest didn't sit well with him.

"Okay." She squeezed his shoulders. "I'll get you a cape."

He kept track of her in the mirror as she walked to a cupboard at the far end of the shop. Moving with graceful efficiency, she pulled out folded towels and a black polyester cape. She'd lived here as many years as he had, but they hadn't met until he'd walked into Tres Beau six months ago.

If she'd always had blue hair, he would have noticed her on the street. Hard to miss something like that. But the color change had happened at the beginning of this year, a Christmas present from Josette.

He'd never run into her at the Choosy Moose, either. He'd asked her once why he hadn't seen her there. Turned out she'd used any spare cash to chip away at the business loan she'd taken out when she and Josette had opened the shop.

A few weeks ago, she'd proudly announced she'd paid off that debt. Her good credit had made her a shoo-in when she'd applied for a home loan last month. Hard-working, disciplined and beautiful—she ticked all the boxes.

She returned, laid the towels on the counter and began tucking his collar under. "I like this shirt."

"Thanks." He preferred T-shirts in the summer, but after he'd experienced Eva's collar-tucking routine back in March, he'd worn a collared shirt to every appointment.

"It brings out the blue in your eyes."

"That's what Sheri said."

"Sheri over at Jeans Junction?"

"Yes, ma'am." They'd gone on a date once to see if friendship could turn into something else. It hadn't, but they'd remained friends.

"She has excellent taste." Eva wrapped a towel around his neck. "Looks new. Did you just buy it?" After snapping the cape in place, she swiveled his chair so he faced away from the mirror.

"Um, yesterday." Hadn't meant to let on about that. But the brush of her fingers against his neck had revved his motor and loosened his tongue.

"Then I'll do my best to keep it dry. Going to the Moose tonight?" She adjusted the chair so he was parallel to the floor, like Rafe.

"Not planning on it." He should have said he was going. That would justify wearing the shirt. But he'd never been good at fibbing.

"Just felt like wearing your new shirt?"

"Right. Gotta break it in, get used to seeing myself in it."

"Well, for what it's worth, I think it suits you."

"Should I wear it on Saturday?"

"Sure, why not?" She'd cushioned the lip of the sink with a towel and, like always, she cupped the back of his head to guide him into position.

"Then I will." Her gentle touch would have been enough to bring him in here on a regular basis even if she'd been lousy at cutting hair. She wasn't, though. He gladly paid more than he would have at the barber shop.

"How's the water temperature?"

"Perfect."

He closed his eyes as she ran warm water over his hair. This next thing was his favorite part, when she worked shampoo into his hair and massaged his scalp.

She had to get close to do it. Her soft breath touched his face, exactly as it would if she'd leaned down to kiss him. He didn't let that concept take hold, though, or he'd be in trouble.

Surrounded by her scent and the warmth of her body, he longed to relax into the pleasure her nimble fingers gave him. He didn't dare. Every appointment provided the same torturous struggle, one he could avoid by ditching this program and going back to the barber shop. He couldn't make himself do it.

"Have you figured out what you're offering?"

Offering? To her? Everything. Oh. For the bachelor auction. They'd each had to dream up something special for the winning bidder. Rafe had quickly claimed an all-day trail ride, which had been Nick's idea, too. Then Leo had taken his other plan, so—

"Nick?"

"Sorry. Had to stop and think."

"Dinner and dancing at the Moose?"

"No, Leo's got that one. We didn't want to be repetitive. Mine is twelve hours of manual labor. Eight in the morning to eight at night, with a couple of breaks for food. Whatever grunt work somebody needs done, I'll handle."

"Wow. I'll bet you could get a lot accomplished in that time." She rinsed the suds out of his hair and stroked conditioner in.

He laughed. "Got some jobs for me?"

"Don't I ever. But with your muscles, you'll probably bring more than I can afford."

"Maybe not." Gratifying that she'd recognized he was in shape. Would she bid on him? What a tantalizing prospect.

"Oh, I think folks will be chomping at the bit to snag a day of hard labor from you. Maybe you shouldn't wear this shirt for the auction, after all."

"Why not?"

Warm water cascaded over his head as she rinsed out the conditioner. "You need to show off your potential. Wear a tight T-shirt instead."

"You think?"

"Definitely. You look great in those." Wrapping a towel around his wet hair, she levered him to a sitting position and turned him to face the mirror.

He used the time to compose himself. At some point in time, she'd admired how he filled out a T-shirt. How cool was that?

Since he wore Western shirts to his appointments, clearly she'd been paying attention when they'd bumped into each other in town this summer. Maybe he wasn't completely out of the running, after all. And maybe he should wear T-shirts to the salon from now on.

He'd been lifting weights for years just so he could eat whatever he wanted, but since meeting Eva he'd made a more concentrated effort to develop his abs. Not that he'd ever expected her to notice.

She'd not only checked him out, she'd love to put his brawn to work. Maybe he'd be lucky and the bidding would stay within her price range. "What is it you need done?"

"To start with, I want to haul everything out of the attic." She rubbed his hair with the towel, tossed it in a hamper and picked up a comb.

"Didn't you just move in?"

"I guess I haven't talked to you since I closed on the house. The bank let me buy the contents, which saved them the trouble of an estate sale. I'd hoped I could do that because I love antiques."

"Bet Miss Barton had a ton of them."

"Yep. She was born in that house. I did her hair for years and she had me over for tea many times." Wielding the scissors with precision, she began snipping away at his hair.

"How old was she?"

"Ninety-seven. I had no idea she didn't have heirs. When I found out the bank would eventually put the house up for sale, I was determined to buy it. The contents were a bonus. I discover something new every day."

"Sounds almost like an archeological dig."

"Exactly. So fun."

"You might want to wait on the attic," Rafe said. "It must be like an oven. Miss Barton didn't believe in A/C."

"It's toasty, all right, especially this week. But I'm dying to know what treasures are packed away up there."

"I would be, too," Nick said.

"If I had you for a day, you could bring it all down for me."

"I doubt that would take all day." And if she didn't win the bidding, he'd offer to do that chore for free.

"Probably not. But if I got lucky and won the bid, I'd send you out to the backyard to dig up rocks. The yard's full of them and I want to plant flowers out there."

"I'm good with rocks."

"I can testify to that," Rafe said. "Nick hauled in the ones we needed for our fire pit behind the bunkhouse. One night we tossed around the idea of building it, and by the next afternoon he had a pile of big rocks, ready to go."

Eva smiled. "Sounds promising."

"You could do something with those rocks." He relished the idea of making something great out of materials on hand.

"Like a fire pit?"

"Maybe, if you want one. You also could create a tiered flower bed. Or maybe a waterfall."

"I'd love a waterfall." She met his gaze in the mirror. "See? You're just the man I need." She didn't say it in a flirty way, as if the words had a double meaning. Instead she said it like they were pals. Good buddies.

Evidently his muscles weren't enough to change that designation. But she was willing to bid on him at the auction. That was a plus. And he'd wear the tightest T-shirt he owned.

2

Eva had found a kindred spirit in Beth Owens, who owned Racy Lace, a lingerie shop on the square. They'd begun meeting for dinner once a week at either Eva's apartment over Tres Beau or Beth's, also located above her shop.

Several months ago, they'd included Fiona Hildebrand, who'd opened a stationery store two doors down from Racy Lace and lived as they did, in rooms over her place of business. The three of them had rotated hosting and tonight was Eva's turn to cook.

She couldn't wait to show them the progress she'd made since they'd first seen the house three weeks ago. That night she'd ordered pizza and served it in the kitchen, the only area besides her bedroom that she'd scrubbed clean.

The house was in decent repair but far from airtight. Dust and cobwebs had collected for more than a year while the Apple Grove Bank had worked through the complexities of an owner who'd died with no will and no heirs. Eva had kept track of the process through a friend at the bank and had been first in line to buy the Victorian.

After a home inspection confirmed the house was structurally sound, Eva had negotiated a lower down payment by agreeing to tackle the cleaning herself. After three weeks of intense labor, the living and dining room were spotless and ready for company.

While the walls, ceilings and furniture had required plenty of vacuuming, everything tucked away in cupboards and drawers had been carefully stored and remained pristine. Winifred Barton had been an excellent housekeeper who'd clearly used and cherished her belongings.

In the living room, two Tiffany-style floor lamps cast jeweled light over worn but elegant furniture from a bygone era. Maybe they were genuine Tiffany and maybe not. Eva didn't much care. They were beautiful.

A lace tablecloth covered the antique dining table and candles flickered in gleaming brass candlesticks. Vintage wine glasses sat at each place, along with silverware that had been stored in a protective chest and had only needed a little polishing to shine like new.

The rumble of a truck sent her to the front window. Instead of walking the four blocks from the square like last time, Beth and Fiona had arrived in Beth's sleek black truck with the Racy Lace logo on the doors.

Eva hurried to the porch as they climbed down, chattering about something she couldn't make out. This week she'd given Beth's brown hair a shorter, sassier cut and it looked darned good, if she did say so. Fiona's ash-blond, shoulder-length style was due for a cut, but she hadn't found the time to come into the salon. Probably explained the ponytail.

Fiona clutched a bottle of white wine. "This is back in stock." She came up the steps and held it out. "I remember we really liked it and then it disappeared."

"It'll go great with dinner." Eva took the chilled bottle. "Is that why you drove instead of walking? You didn't want the wine to get warm?"

"Or us," Beth said. "Last time it felt almost like fall and the walk was nice. This week, not so much."

"Four blocks isn't popping-over distance like when I lived on the square. That's the only downside."

"It's okay," Beth said. "This house was calling your name."

"It sure was." Fiona laughed. "Even I heard it. *Eeee-vaaa. Forget the moneeee. You neeed meee.*"

Eva snorted. "Yep, I'm mortgaged up to my eyebrows, but I don't care. The house is awesome. We're eating in style in the dining room tonight, so be impressed. Be very impressed."

"And I smell your famous spaghetti sauce." Fiona started for the door. "Let's open the wine before the chill wears off."

"I'll handle that," Eva said. "You two go admire all the work I've done." She followed them into the house and ducked into the kitchen while they continued into the living room and the adjacent dining room.

Their loud chorus of *oooo* and *aaahhhh* made her giggle. "Okay, that's enough." She pulled a platter of antipasto out of the fridge and carried it and the open wine bottle into the dining room. "Don't overdo it." She set down the platter and poured the wine.

"I didn't have to fake it." Beth turned to survey the living room. "Both rooms look gorgeous. Better than I expected after seeing it three weeks ago. I notice you found a spot for the painting."

"Doesn't it look great there?" The painting had been her Aunt Sally's favorite, a laughing woman in a summer dress running through a field of wildflowers. She'd hung it over the antique loveseat.

"Perfect." Fiona nodded enthusiastically, making her ponytail swing. "And by the way, are the wine glasses on the dining table valuable antiques? I'm asking for a friend." She grinned at Beth.

"That was a one-time situation. I was upset and got careless with my wine glass." Beth glanced at Eva. "But just so I know, *are* those priceless?" She pointed to the mismatched wineglasses on the table. "Like, is there a one-of-a-kind Baccarat in the mix?"

"No. I've found a few things in the china cabinet that might qualify as priceless, but the glasses aren't."

"Sell the priceless stuff online," Fiona said. "With the right ad copy, you might get—"

"Ack, blasphemy!" Eva waved her hands in the air. "I didn't buy this place to bleed off its assets. Unless I positively hate something, it stays. I don't care what it's worth."

Fiona's eyes rounded. "How can you not care? You're more cash-strapped than we are now that you've bought—"

"My old house back." She glanced from Beth to Fiona. "I've never said that out loud. Does it sound crazy?"

Beth shook her head. "Not to me. Judging from the pictures you showed us, this house looks a lot like the one you grew up in."

"Forget what I said." Fiona came over and gave her a hug. "I was hung up on being practical."

"Which this house isn't." Eva cast a loving gaze over the two rooms she'd finished. "I don't care. It feels like home already." She gestured to the table. "Let's sit."

"You should take the head of this grand old table." Beth moved around to pull out the chair on her left. "Wow, the upholstery on the seat is in great shape. Comfy, too."

"Which means it's been reupholstered." Eva claimed the spot Beth had assigned her.

"I love a dining chair with arms." Fiona settled into the one on Eva's right. "You can relax into it."

"I guess that's true. I was so busy cleaning I didn't take the time to try out the chairs. They're cushy."

Beth glanced at her. "Is this the first meal you've eaten in here?"

"As a matter of fact. Eating alone at a table for eight feels weird. I've been using the one in the kitchen."

"I'm honored we're the first guests to enjoy this great setting." Fiona picked up her wine glass. "To many more dinners in this lovely room."

"I'll drink to that." Beth clinked glasses with Eva and Fiona before taking her first sip. "And I can't wait to dive into this antipasto platter." She set down her glass and helped herself to some provolone, olives and artichoke hearts. "Are you two still up for the Raptors Rise benefit on Saturday?"

"I am." Fiona served herself. "I'll close the shop at noon." She glanced at Eva. "How about you?"

"We're also closing at noon. I'll need a few minutes to get ready, but I can meet you guys about twelve-thirty."

"I was hoping you both were still going," Beth said. "I can use the moral support."

Eva had a bite halfway to her mouth and put it down again. "You've decided to bid on Jared?"

"Yep." Beth took a hefty swallow of wine. "Might as well find out if he's into me at all."

Eva gazed at her friend. "Whenever I see you two together, he acts like he is."

"Then why hasn't he suggested going for a drink at the Moose after work? He almost always closes Logan's Leather the same time as I lock up Racy Lace."

"Hm." Fiona gazed at her. "Why haven't you asked *him* to go for drinks?"

She sighed. "I'm too chicken. If he said no, I'd still have to see him all the time. That would be awkward."

Fiona took another helping of the antipasto. "But you're not too chicken to bid on him at the auction?"

"That's different. I'm helping him raise money for Raptors Rise. We're doing our civic duty."

Eva smiled. "So selfless. Where would he take you if you win?"

"To the re-opened drive-in movie theater."

"Nice."

"I like the idea. It's retro. Casual yet cozy. We're not staring at each other over a table and wondering what to say. Even if he doesn't ask me out after that, it won't be so pointed. I just need to win the bid."

"Don't worry," Fiona said. "We'll cheer you on as you blithely empty your checking account." She looked over at Eva. "Am I right?"

"Absolutely. I, on the other hand, don't want to get carried away when I bid on Nick Le Grande."

Beth's eyebrows lifted. "Nick? Do you like him? I don't remember you ever saying—"

"Of course I like him, but I don't *like* him. I just want what he's offering—twelve hours of manual labor. I don't want to exceed my budget, though, so if I get bidding fever, hold me back."

"Aha!" Fiona looked up at the ceiling. "This is all about that interesting stuff in the attic."

"Bingo. And when he's brought everything downstairs, I'll send him out to the backyard to dig up rocks. When I mentioned that, he suggested using the rocks for a waterfall. I think he's interested in helping me build it."

Beth's   gaze   grew   speculative. "Considering the forecast for Saturday and your lack of A/C, he'll probably have his shirt off by the time he's digging up rocks and building a waterfall."

"So what?"

"*So what*? Hey, you may not *like* him." She made air quotes. "But that doesn't mean you can't take him a refreshing beverage if he's working shirtless in your backyard."

"I probably will, now that you mention it. But I'd do it to keep him hydrated, not so I can admire his muscles."

Fiona reached over and patted her arm. "You're missing the point. Nick has a nice body and likely worked hard to make it that way."

"That may be true, but—"

"Trust me, he won't be offended if you give him an admiring glance or two. He might be disappointed if you don't."

"Oh, for heaven's sake. He won't be disappointed because we don't have that kind of relationship. We're just friends."

"Is that how he'll see it if you bid on him? A bachelor auction has a sexy vibe."

"Maybe for Beth and Jared, but not for me and Nick. He knows exactly why I'm doing it. We talked about it when he came in for a haircut today."

"Okay, then." Fiona shrugged. "Maybe the two of you will spend a sweaty day together and still be just good buddies at the end of it." She glanced at Beth. "What do you think?"

Beth smiled at Eva. "I think I want a play-by-play on Monday morning. You've got your dream house. Now you need to find your dream man."

"Nah, I don't believe in that stuff."

"What stuff?"

"You know." Eva waved a hand in the air. "Someday my prince will show up, sweep me off my feet and we'll live happily ever after."

"I'm confused," Beth said. "Weren't you lusting after CJ a couple of months ago?"

"I was, but now that I see how happy he is with a fiancée and a baby on the way, I realize he would have been the exact wrong guy for me. I don't want to get tied down."

"Why not?"

"Didn't we talk about this one time?"

Beth shook her head. "Not that I remember. Fi, does this sound familiar?"

"Sort of. I remember something about not getting married, but I didn't think that meant never."

Eva shrugged. "I just don't see myself making that commitment. Aunt Sally was happy being single. She had boyfriends but didn't live with or marry any of them. Josette seems perfectly fine on her own. Ed does, too. I think it's the way to go."

"I'll be darned." Beth gazed at her. "I thought for sure buying this place was a first step to finding Mister Right and filling the house with kids."

"Nope. Aunt Sally didn't feel that need. Miss Barton didn't, either. And neither do I."

3

Nick's T-shirt was damp with sweat as he and Rafe exited Ed's indoor riding arena. Normally her arena served as a barrel-racing practice site for the Babes on Buckskins, a close-knit group of women that included Nick and Rafe's boss, Henri Fox.

Tonight, it would be the scene of Apple Grove's first-ever bachelor auction. Because the participants were all cowboys, they'd be showcased on horseback.

The building had A/C, but Nick had put effort into his riding during the run-through for tonight's event. And—might as well admit it—he had a bad case of jitters. Rafe looked uneasy, too.

Ed came out with them, using the excuse that she needed some fresh air. Nick wasn't fooled. She'd noticed he and Rafe had stage fright. They were in for a pep talk.

The area between the arena and Ed's palatial ranch house bustled with activity connected to the Raptors Rise fundraising event— vendors and townspeople in a festive mix.

Ed surveyed the scene before turning to Nick and Rafe. "Forgive me for being blunt, but you boys seem uncomfortable with the bachelor auction concept."

Nick heaved a sigh. "I want to help out, but you're right. I'm nervous as hell."

"I wasn't nervous until that rehearsal," Rafe said. "Leo and Garrett seemed fine with galloping around the arena, showing off. Teague and Logan, too. As for Ben, he's always been cool. But I—"

"Don't be fooled." Ed shoved her hands in the pockets of her jeans. "Ben's a showman at heart, which is why the Choosy Moose has done so well over the years. Jared may be okay with it, too. But the others are just better at disguising their feelings than you are."

"The thing is, we're cowboys." Nick took his hat off and ran his fingers through his hair. "Not performers."

"That hits the nail on the head." Rafe grimaced. "Then there's the whole bidding thing. Like I'm a prize bull or stallion."

Ed smiled. "Some men would love that comparison."

"Not me."

"The key is to relax and have fun with it. You boys aren't used to being in the spotlight."

Nick took a deep breath. "That's for sure."

"Every performer I know, including me, gets a touch of nerves as they wait for their cue. But when they get out there and the crowd is clapping and cheering, they're fine. You will be, too."

Rafe shook his head. "I seriously doubt that. Whose idea was this, anyway?"

Ed was a tall woman, but she still had to look up to make eye contact with Rafe, who stood six-six in his bare feet, six-eight in boots. "Ben suggested it."

"Ben?" Nick frowned. "Why would he—"

"Henri." Amusement danced in her eyes and she looked much younger than eighty-five. "Not *just* because of her. A bachelor auction's a proven moneymaker. As a bonus, Henri will feel obligated to bid on him because Raptors Rise is her pet project. And he'll finally get a date with her after all these years."

"Yeah," Nick said, "but not if somebody outbids her."

Ed's eyebrows rose. "Can you picture that happening? You do know Henri Fox, right?"

Rafe chuckled. "That'll be fun to watch. Knowing this tickles me enough I might just get over myself and have a good time."

"Yeah, me too." Nick grinned. "Gotta hand it to Ben. Well-played."

"I'm glad you both approve. Where are you off to now that the rehearsal's over?"

Rafe glanced toward a spacious tent marked with a hanging wooden sign etched with someone's signature. "I was planning to check out Quinn Sawyer's scratchboard art. I heard he brought up his Birds of Prey collection."

"Great idea. I didn't get a chance to check out his work when we went down to Eagles Nest for Seth's wedding. Mind if I tag along?"

"Glad to have you. Nick? You in?"

"Why not? I didn't get to see any of his stuff when we were down there, either. Then again, I was distracted by all the goodies from the bakery. What was the name of it?"

"Pie in the Sky. Can't believe you don't remember the name. You were so in love with it, I wondered if we'd have to leave you in Eagles Nest."

"Nah, my heart belongs to the Apple Barrel's signature pie, but I can still taste those brownies."

"Now you sound like your old self, bro." Rafe led the way to Quinn Sawyer's tent.

An attractive woman with silver streaks in her dark hair stood near the entrance. Had to be Kendra McGavin. Her smile lit up her blue eyes. "Rafe, isn't it? And..."

"Nick Le Grande, ma'am." Nick tipped his hat. "And this is Ed Vidal. She shortened her—"

"In January I was still using Edna." She stepped forward and shook hands with Kendra. "I like Ed better."

"I remember you well. You're the champion barrel racer. I normally use Kendra, but when my first grandchild was born I decided to be Granny Ken. Shakes things up a bit."

Ed smiled. "Always a good thing." She glanced toward the rear of the tent. "Looks like Quinn is involved with a customer. We can just browse until he's done."

Kendra lowered her voice. "She's not a customer. He'd probably welcome the interruption."

Quinn, a tall, very fit cowboy with graying hair, worried the brim of his Stetson as he held a hushed but tense discussion with the woman who faced him. Her hairstyle and tailored Western wear had a timeless quality that made it tough to guess her age. But her stance telegraphed determination.

Rafe frowned. "Is she some kind of groupie?"

"And what's she doing with a bullhorn?" Nick peered at her. "If she's not from around here, I can't imagine why she'd have—"

"I think I know her." Ed studied the woman. "What's her name?"

"Ellie Mae—"

"Oh, my God." Ed's eyes widened. "It's Ellie Mae Stockton. The bullhorn should have tipped me off. What's she up to?"

"She wants to stand outside the tent and drum up business."

Ed glanced around the deserted tent. "You do seem short on customers."

"We had plenty this morning when it was cooler. Quinn's sold some pricey items and he's satisfied with the donation he'll be able to make. He doesn't want her out there hawking his art. That's not how he presents himself."

"Judging from his expression, he's being way too nice." Ed continued to watch the pair. "That woman has spent decades in the film industry. She has the soul of a circus barker and a will of iron."

Nick perked up. He'd always been fascinated by Ed's connection to Hollywood. "Is that where you know her from?"

"Oh, yeah. Directors loved putting a bullhorn in her hand and letting her direct the troops. She's the unstoppable person you want in your lifeboat even if she's a royal pain in the ass. She'll be out there with her bullhorn promoting Quinn's art or know the reason why."

"He'll hate that."

"Then stand aside, Granny Ken." Ed threw her shoulders back and lifted her chin. She looked a lot taller than she had a few seconds ago. "I'm going in."

Nick elbowed Rafe in the ribs and winked. "Let's get closer. This'll be good."

Kendra blinked. "What's she going to do?"

"I'm not sure, but I've seen her strike that pose a few times before. It's like the moment when Superman rips open his shirt. She goes from being a perky senior citizen to Edna Jane Vidal, world-champion barrel racer."

"Then yeah, let's get closer." Kendra waved them forward.

Ed lengthened her stride and spoke with the authority of a drill sergeant. "As I live and breathe, if it isn't Ellie Mae Stockton!"

The other woman whirled. "Edna?"

"Who else?" She raised her arms. "The queen of the arena is in the building!"

Ellie Mae lifted the bullhorn and bellowed into it. "Ladies and gentlemen, may I present the one, the only, Edna Jane Vidal!" She laid the bullhorn on a nearby display table and rushed forward with a loud whoop.

Laughing like teenagers, the two women exchanged vigorous hip bumps and an elaborate fist and hand-slapping routine, clearly a ritual from their shared past. At the end of it, Ed gave

Ellie Mae a light punch on the arm. "Whatcha doing with that bullhorn, girl? Causing trouble as usual?"

"Trying to, Edna Jane, except this gentleman is resisting my best efforts." She swept an arm toward Quinn. "Talk some sense into him, please. He's got amazing artwork, but he doesn't understand you gotta sell it. Know what I mean?"

"Sure do. Nothing wrong with pimping yourself out for a good cause."

Quinn sent a silent plea in Kendra's direction and she started forward.

"But, alternatively…" Ed positioned herself to block Kendra's progress. "You could be wasting your talents in this case. Especially when you're desperately needed elsewhere."

Ellie Mae folded her arms and narrowed her eyes. "Don't try to distract me, Edna Jane. I'll be very good for Quinn's bottom line, which will be very good for Raptors Rise."

"I don't doubt that for a minute. But hear me out. I assume you're aware of our signature event tonight?"

"Who isn't? I have my eye on the owner of the Choosy Moose. He's hot."

"A word to the wise, Ben could never keep up with you. Besides, I have a much tastier plan. Why be stuck in the crowd tonight when you could be up on stage hob-knobbing with *all* those gorgeous cowboys?"

"You want me to be the stage manager?"

"Even better, I want you in charge of the entire shootin' match. I was going to claim that role, but—much as I hate to say so—you're a better fit. How would you like to be our auctioneer?"

Color bloomed in Ellie Mae's cheeks and a shiver of excitement rippled through her slim body. Then she took a slow breath and studied her manicured nails. "I might consider it." She looked up. "Will there be an after-party?"

"Definitely. A chance for the bachelors and the high bidders to mingle and for you to shine. It'll be up at my house."

"That's *your* house?"

Ed nodded, a trace of smug satisfaction in her gaze.

"So you're the *Ed* I've been hearing about, the one who owns this ranch? I thought it belonged to some guy."

"I shortened my name for dramatic effect. Do we have a deal?"

"Oh, we have a deal, chica. And we need to talk so I can find out how winning some trophies and playing bit parts in a few Westerns resulted in *this.*" She spread her arms.

"Compound interest and solid stocks."

"Talk to me, girlfriend."

"I will, but first we'll head over to the arena so you can familiarize yourself with the setup."

"Good. I always insist on that. This isn't amateur hour."

"Not with you at the helm. After we check out the stage and lights, we'll grab a six-pack of hard cider and I'll tell you all."

"Excellent."

Ed tipped her hat to Quinn and Kendra. "Great seeing you two again."

Quinn stepped forward and offered his hand. "Thank you, ma'am. Ellie Mae, you'll make a terrific auctioneer."

"And you're going to regret letting Edna Jane steal me away."

"Don't worry," Kendra said. "If business doesn't pick up, I'll send the Whine and Cheese Club out with sandwich boards."

Ed brightened. "The Whine and Cheese Club is here? How did I miss that?"

"We've kept our presence low-key. Didn't want to step on any toes, namely those of the Babes on Buckskins. This is your event, but if you need any—"

"Oh, we can use you—all of you—as facilitators. Please tell anyone who's willing to help to show up at the arena around six."

"Will do."

Ed turned to Rafe and Nick. "Ellie Mae, allow me to introduce two members of the Buckskin Brotherhood, Nick Le Grande and Rafe Banner."

Nick and Rafe whipped off their hats and held them against their chests as they each murmured a polite greeting.

Ellie Mae gave them an appreciative once-over. "Buckskin Brotherhood, huh? That sounds sexy. I recognize both of you from the bachelor auction flyer, but you're even better looking in person."

Nick flushed. "Thank you, ma'am."

"So, Nick, what would you like me to say about you before the bidding starts?"

He blurted out the first thing that came to him. "I'm strong as an ox."

"I'll just bet you are. You're straining the seams of your shirt. Your physical strength is obvious, but what about your character? Who are you inside?"

He drew a complete blank.

"I can tell you," Rafe said. "You can count on this guy. He'll be there for you, no matter what."

"That's lovely."

Nick glanced at him. "Thanks, bro."

"What about you, Rafe? What should I say about you?"

"I wouldn't hurt a fly."

"That's commendable since clearly you could squash most things flat if you wanted. People, too, I'll bet."

"I don't, though."

"But it's not like he's harmless," Nick said. "Go after something or someone Rafe loves and you'd better watch out."

"A protector." Ellie Mae nodded. "Excellent. If the other bachelors are anything like you guys, we'll raise a ton of money for Raptors Rise tonight."

4

Country music poured from the speakers mounted in a surround-sound configuration in the arena. Finding a seat on the crowded bleachers wasn't easy. Eva finally spotted an opening five rows up that would work.

She pointed it out to her friends and led the way, excusing herself as she edged past other spectators to get to it.

"Well done." Fiona plopped down on the seat next to Eva. "This is crazy. Are all these people here to bid?"

"I doubt it." Beth settled next to Fiona. "I think most folks are just curious." She took out her phone and silenced it. "Phones, everybody."

Eva silenced hers. "And some will have deeper pockets than mine. But I'll stick to my limit and see what happens."

"Well, I've decided not to bid on Jared at all." Beth gave them a look clearly designed to end the discussion.

"You'd better have a really good reason," Fiona said, "or I'll point at you and start clucking like a chicken."

"I have a great reason. If he wanted to ask me out, he would have done it already. It's been a year since I opened my shop next to his and we decided to cross-promote. He's had ample opportunity to—"

"As Fiona mentioned before," Eva said, "so have you. We're past the days when the guy has to make the first move."

"But I'm the new person in town. Shouldn't he be the one to—" She broke off as Fiona started making clucking noises. "How many guys have *you* asked out since you arrived in Apple Grove, Miss Fiona?"

"None, yet, but I—"

"Did you bring your checkbook?"

"It's always in my wallet, but I'm not going to—"

"Why not?" Beth stared her down. "What better time to take the plunge than tonight, when the money supports a worthy cause?"

"I'm supporting it in other ways. I bought one of Lucy's sketches."

"So did Eva and I, but they weren't expensive. The bachelor auction is the big money maker."

"But you just said you weren't biding on Jared, so you're not contributing to the cause, either. If I'm doing it, you're doing it."

Beth sighed. "All right. I'll risk making a fool of myself. You need to pick somebody."

"I didn't even look at this thing." Fiona pulled the flyer out of her purse and consulted it. "I don't know any of these guys, except Jared, of course. Stationery shops don't attract male customers, as a rule."

"I wouldn't know them, either," Eva said, "except they come in for haircuts. If we all went to the Moose on a regular basis, we'd—"

"I can't justify it," Fiona said. "Getting that business off the ground is more important than meeting sexy cowboys."

"Clearly they don't come into Racy Lace, either," Beth said. "Eva, you have the inside track. Who should she bid on?"

"Well, I—"

"What about him?" Fiona tapped on a picture. "Leo Marston is gorgeous. I've never dated anybody that handsome."

Eva glanced at the picture. "He'd look even better if he'd get his hair cut at Tres Beau."

"I thought they all did, now."

"All of them except Leo. He's the only Buckskin Brotherhood holdout."

"Is it because Tres Beau is more expensive? I don't want to bid on a tightwad, especially since we'd be going on a dinner date."

"It's not the money. Nick says it's almost as if Leo resents being so handsome. He constantly downplays his appearance."

"I'm intrigued." Fiona tucked the flyer back in her purse. "A handsome guy who's not full of himself. I'll bid on him, but I refuse to empty my checking account."

"I'm not doing that for Jared, either."

"Should we all agree on a set amount?" Eva had one in mind, but she'd let them chime in.

"Here's a reasonable benchmark," Beth said. "The price of a cut, color and tip at Tres Beau."

"That works." Eva had intended to spend twice that. Nick would probably bring a lot more, which meant if she stuck with their agreed-upon limit she wouldn't win the bid.

"Where do you suppose they're keeping the guys?" Beth scanned the arena. "You'd think they'd want them out here where we could eyeball them."

"Not necessarily." Eva looked around, too. "They could be hiding in plain sight, but I don't think so. My guess is they're tucked away somewhere to build the suspense. Henri's going up to the mic. We must be getting close."

Fiona leaned toward Eva. "I want to be Henri Fox when I grow up. I've always been self-conscious about being tall, but look at how she carries herself."

"She's regal. All the Babes walk tall and proud, for that matter."

"Lucy hasn't got that down yet," Beth said.

"Yeah, but she's shorter." Eva admired the heck out of Lucy. "And a newbie. Give her another year as a Babe and she'll be strutting around like the rest of them."

Beth laughed. "She needs to get platform boots."

"Good evening, ladies and gentlemen!" Henri's clear voice quieted the crowd immediately. "Welcome to Apple Grove's first-ever bachelor auction!" Cheers and applause followed. She waited for it to die down. "I'm sure you're eager to start the bidding on our dashingly handsome bachelors. First, though, let's hear from the founder of Raptors Rise, Zane McGavin!"

"Hey, he's cute," Fiona murmured as the crowd applauded for Zane. She pulled out the flyer. "Is he one of the—"

"He's married," Eva said.

"Shoot."

Zane acknowledged the crowd's enthusiasm with a brilliant smile. Then he nudged back his hat with his thumb. "Folks, I can't tell you how much that welcome means to me. I dreamed about creating a sanctuary for birds of prey when I was a teenager. Back then I thought establishing Raptors Rise in Eagles Nest would be the ultimate high."

He took a breath. "Expanding the project to Apple Grove has shown me that I didn't dream big enough. I'm grateful to Henri Fox for donating the land and to all of you for generously supporting a second location for Raptors Rise."

The crowd responded with more energetic applause.

Zane's voice became gruff with emotion. "Because of you, the magnificent eagles, hawks, owls and falcons who live in this valley will have a sanctuary where injuries are healed and orphaned chicks get a second chance. The information center will educate and advocate for the birds and a sustainable environment that will benefit us all. Thank you from the bottom of my heart." With a tip of his hat, he stepped back from the mic as the crowd roared its approval.

Henri returned. "Thank you, Zane. Beautifully stated."

Fiona nudged Eva again. "Is he *happily* married?"

"Very." Eva grinned at her. "Put your tongue back in your mouth."

"Before we start," Henri said, "I need to make a few more introductions. Please hold your applause until I'm finished. Our auctioneer will be Ellie Mae Stockton, a veteran events coordinator from Eagles Nest who has a background in the film industry."

A woman dressed in tailored jeans, high-heeled boots and a sequined black Western shirt came forward.

Beth glanced at Eva. "Do you know her?"

"Haven't a clue. I heard that Ed was going to be the auctioneer."

"Our facilitators," Henri said, "include our own Babes on Buckskins." She gestured toward the six women who stepped up on stage. "We'll be assisting our bachelors."

The Babes received a warm welcome from the stands.

"Joining us from Eagles Nest," Henri continued, "are the six women of the Whine and Cheese Club, staunch supporters of Raptors Rise. They'll escort our top bidders to the Winner's Circle where winner and bachelor can meet and discuss their planned activity."

"Yikes." Fiona sucked in a breath. "I didn't expect we'd come face-to-face *tonight.*"

"No chickening out," Beth said. "You promised."

"It'll be fine," Eva said. "Just confirm the arrangements and thank Leo for volunteering to do this. No big deal."

"Easy for you to say." Fiona gave her a look. "You're just hiring a handyman. He's not taking you on a date."

"True." Instead, in the unlikely event she won, she'd have a muscular cowboy tromping around in her house and working shirtless in her backyard tomorrow. For twelve hours.

As the music swelled and the crowd grew restless with anticipation, she faced the truth of Fiona's comment. A bachelor auction had a sexy vibe.

Oh, well, didn't matter. She wouldn't win.

5

Let's get on with it. Nick's plan to relax and have fun disintegrated under the pressure of his impending performance. The double doors at the back of the arena were open a crack so the bachelors could hear what was going on inside.

Each of them held the reins of the horse Ed had provided for their use, except for Jared, who'd brought his gray gelding. Nick had a big caramel-colored palomino named Thor. At least he'd make his entrance on a showstopper horse.

Half of the guys stood to one side of the doors and half on the other, staying in the shadow of the building. Even when the doors opened, only the cowboy riding through would be visible.

Ben had appointed himself head wrangler. Fine with Nick. Ben had volunteered to kick off the action and demonstrate how simple it would be. Yeah. Jumping off a cliff was simple, too.

Nobody was talking. Most of the guys had a hand on their horse's muzzle to help keep them quiet. The idea was to maintain an element of surprise, at least until Ben charged through the back door.

Nick was the only one rocking a T-shirt, although it wasn't the same one he'd worn today. Like everyone else, he'd brought a change of clothes and his shaving kit.

Teague, Ed's wrangler, had a house on the property. He'd made it available so the guys could shower, shave and put on clean clothes.

Nick's T-shirt choice had worried him some when the others had busted out their fancy shirts with embroidery on the yokes and collars. Too late to do anything about it, though.

The back door opened and Ed slipped through. "We've added a wrinkle to build suspense. For each entrance, we'll start your music soft and the Whine and Cheese ladies will do a little dancing. Then Ellie Mae will call out your name, we'll crank up the music and you'll barrel through the doorway. Everybody got that?"

All the guys nodded.

"Ben, take Ranger out about ten yards so you'll have a good head of steam when you burst on the scene. The rest of you follow his example when it's your turn." She glanced at her phone. "Two minutes. Then Josette and I will open the doors. Thanks for doing this." She ducked back into the arena.

Nick gulped. Not long now. He was third in the lineup, better than first and preferable to last, Rafe's position. He glanced over and gave Rafe a thumbs-up. The big guy responded in kind. He looked a little green around the gills, but maybe that was a trick of the light.

The opening to Ben's chosen song, Toby Keith's *How Do You Like Me Now?* filtered out through the crack in the door. Then Ellie Mae Stockton's voice rang out. "Give it up for the owner of the Choosy Moose, Ben Malone!"

Ed and Josette threw back the doors. With a whoop, Ben slapped Ranger on the rump with his hat. As the sound system belted out the tune, the powerful bay leaped forward and dashed through the doorway at a full gallop. The open door gave Nick a partial view as Ben circled the arena, standing in his stirrups, his hat lifted in salute to the cheering crowd, a huge grin on his face.

"Damn," Rafe muttered from behind him. "He's having a blast."

"Maybe you will, too, bro."

"Fat chance."

The music cut off and Ben wheeled Ranger to face the bleachers while Ellie Mae talked him up. Then she started the bidding.

The pace was brisk and the amount kept climbing. Nick turned to Rafe, eyebrows lifted. "Don't hear Henri."

"Nope."

Then she jumped in, her voice carrying over the rest. The amount she called out was huge, enough to bring a collective gasp from the onlookers.

"Going once." Ellie Mae paused. "Going twice... *sold* to Henri Fox! Henri, go meet your bachelor in the Winners' Circle."

Leo chuckled. "Sure wish I could see Ben's face right now."

"I'm happy for him," Nick said.

"And her," Rafe said. "She really should give Ben a shot. They'd go good together."

"Maybe now they'll figure that out." Nick's tension eased some. Henri and Ben would make a good match. But his anxiety came roaring back when Ed and Josette signaled to Jared.

He mounted Shadow and guided the horse to the spot Ben had vacated. The intro to Alabama's *Mountain Music* was easy to hear now that the doors stood open. Nick had a glimpse of the Whine and Cheese ladies doing a line dance.

Then Ellie Mae came on. "Make some noise for the owner of Logan's Leather, Jared Logan!"

The music blared as Jared and Shadow bolted through the door. Putting the reins in his teeth, Jared lifted his hands over his head and clapped in time to the music. The crowd joined in, clearly having fun.

"The guy has skills," Rafe muttered.

"Uh-huh." Nick's nerves were jangling and he didn't catch much of what Ellie Mae said about Jared. Or much of the bidding, either. Heart thudding, he mounted up when Ed and Josette signaled to him.

His song was *Stay a Little Longer* by the Brothers Osborne, a tune chosen because it had a line about T-shirts. Seemed to take forever to position Thor at the starting line and even longer while the opening bars of the song played.

Ellie Mae's voice nearly gave him a heart attack. "Let's show some love to bachelor Nick La Grande!"

Nick dug his heels into Thor's ribs and the palomino exploded, hurtling through the open doors. Nick hunched over the horse's neck, the cream-colored mane slapping him in the face as they took that circuit at a breakneck pace.

The music cut off and he pulled up in a cloud of dust, breathing hard. Thor snorted and pranced with impatience, wanting another run. Nick murmured to the big palomino and stroked his sweat-darkened neck.

"What a thrilling entrance, Nick." Ellie Mae turned toward him and blew him a kiss before facing the spectators again. "As the program states, Nick is offering twelve hours of manual labor, and you can see for yourselves he's up to the job. Wooooee!"

Nick's face heated but he didn't duck his head. The Babes had emphasized during the rehearsal that hiding behind a hat was a no-no. *Look them in the eye and smile.* And he did, although his smile likely was more of a grimace.

"I have something else to tell you about Bachelor Number Three, intel I obtained from one of Nick's best friends. He said, and I quote, *you can count on this guy. He'll be there for you, no matter what.* With Nick Le Grande you get strength of body *and* strength of character. That's a bargain at any price. What am I bid for this amazing cowboy?"

A woman called out a significant amount that made him blink in surprise. Eva? He spotted her blue hair and sure enough, she was on her feet. Then someone topped her bid. *Sit down, Eva. Save your money.*

Instead she bid over the other lady. One of the servers at the Moose upped the ante. Eva hung in, raising her bid. Nick looked straight at her and gave a slight shake of his head. She looked right back and smiled.

The first lady added more money to the pot and still Eva remained on her feet. The bidding kept on, going ever higher. A woman next to her, clearly a friend, grabbed her arm and tried to coax her back to her seat. She was having none of it.

The bidding became more spirited as the amount spiraled into the ridiculous zone. He should have talked her out of this when he'd had the chance. Maybe *now* she'd drop out.

Instead she doubled the previous bid. Sheesh.

As the other two took their seats, she did a fist pump and grinned in triumph. His heart squeezed. He would work himself to the bone for her tomorrow. Even so, his labor wasn't worth a third of what she'd just spent.

"Nick."

He glanced down as someone wiggled his stirrup.

Peggy gazed up at him, her expression sympathetic. "You need to dismount, cowboy," she murmured.

"Yes, ma'am." He swung down. "What should I—"

"I'll take Thor. Pam will escort you to the Winners' Circle."

"Winners' Circle?" He handed her the reins as Pam came toward him.

"Didn't we tell you about that?"

"If you did, I spaced it."

"We might have come up with the idea after we brainstormed with the Whine and Cheese Club. The Babes are escorting the bachelors to the Winners' Circle and the Whine and Cheese ladies are doing the same with the winning bidders."

"Where is it?"

"Behind the bleachers," Pam said. "Come with me. Nice job, by the way."

"I didn't do anything." He fell into step beside her.

"You showed up. And you delivered. We didn't realize until the run-through that some of you guys were scared stiff."

"Could you tell just now?"

"Nope. Your cheeks got a little pink 'cause you were embarrassed, but that was cute."

"What's supposed to happen in this Winners' Circle?"

"You meet with your winning bidder, in your case, Eva. Deidre's going up into the bleachers to escort her down."

"So I see." Deidre, a buxom woman with fiery red hair, was standing in the bleacher aisle waiting for Eva to make her way over.

"Have you met any of the Whine and Cheese ladies?"

"Yes, ma'am, at Seth's wedding. Deidre's a little crazy, but in a good way."

"I couldn't have said it better. Those women are aces in my book. We've already invited them to drive up for our next sleepover."

"Heaven help us."

"Hey, we'll keep things circumspect."

He chuckled. "Sure. Because you always do."

"Nick Le Grande, how you talk."

"Just telling it like it is. Those sleepovers are already wild." Adrenaline continued to race through his system and joking around with her helped calm him down.

"Yeah, well, when you're right, you're right."

"Will you give us some advance warning? Just so the Brotherhood will be standing by in case things get totally out of hand."

"When have we ever had to call you boys to the rescue?"

"Let's see... the skinny dipping in the creek episode, the stargazing on the roof incident, and the—"

"Yeah, yeah." She laughed. "Point taken."

"So I meet up with Eva in the Winners' Circle. What then? Are you gonna hang roses around our necks?"

"Wish we'd thought of it."

"Glad you didn't."

"Mostly you drink apple cider and eat munchies with the other bachelors and winners. Henri and Ben are back there with Jared and Beth."

"Beth who?"

"Owens. Her shop is next to Jared's."

"Oh, yeah. Racy Lace."

"Ever been in?"

"No, ma'am."

"Well, if you ever need to buy something sexy for a special lady, that's the place. And speaking of sexy, did you wash that shirt in hot water to make it shrink?"

"I washed it in hot water by accident. Figured I'd use it for work. Then Eva said I should wear something snug, so I did."

"Eva was right." She rounded the bleachers and gestured to a roped off area with a sparkly sign that said *Winners' Circle*. "This is where you'll be hanging out, and here come Henri and Ben to greet you. I need to skedaddle. Congrats on a great ride." She gave his shoulder a squeeze.

"Hey, son." Henri walked toward him, a bottle of cider in her hand and a smiling Ben by her side. "That was terrific."

"Thanks, Henri."

"Good job, buddy." Ben shook his hand.

"You're the flashy one, Ben, standing in the stirrups, doffing your hat to the crowd. Ever done any stunt riding?"

"When I was younger and dumber."

Henri flashed him a grin. "And now you're older and...."

"Still dumb. Halfway into that stunt my left knee threatened to give out." He winked at Henri. "But I got lucky."

She arched an eyebrow. "We'll see about that."

Nick choked back a laugh. Henri was flirting. Never thought he'd see the day. Promised to be entertaining as hell.

Henri glanced at him. "So who won the bidding? We couldn't hear very well back there."

"Eva."

"Eva won?" Beth had come out of the Winners' Circle with Jared and she hurried toward him.

"Yes, ma'am."

"Awesome."

"Hey, Nick," Jared said, "do you know Beth? Her shop is—"

"Next to yours." He tipped his hat. "Pleased to meet you."

"Same here, Nick."

"Unfortunately, I've never been inside your place."

"No worries. Guess you haven't had a reason."

"No, ma'am." Still didn't.

She glanced over his shoulder and waved. "Here comes your winner."

Nick turned. Eva's smile had a touch of—what was the word? Bravado. Like she'd done something outrageous and was daring him to comment on it. So maybe he wouldn't.

Deidre had an arm around her waist. "Nick Le Grande, it's my privilege to present Eva Kilpatrick, your winning bidder."

"Thank you, ma'am. Eva and I—"

"I'm aware you two know each other, but I love my job and I'm going to do it whether you need me to or not."

Nick grinned at Eva and the light of challenge in her eyes softened. Good. If they could muddle through this part together, it might be fun, after all.

Deidre pulled a rolled piece of paper from her pocket, unfurled it with a flourish and began to read. "Eva Kilpatrick, you have this night purchased one of our esteemed bachelors, Nick Le Grande. He's pledged to give you twelve hours of manual labor beginning tomorrow morning at eight sharp. Is that correct?"

"Yes."

"Excellent. Nick Le Grande, you have participated in this bachelor auction with the understanding that you will donate twelve hours of manual labor to the winning bidder, Eva Kilpatrick, such labor to begin at eight sharp tomorrow morning. Is that correct?"

"Yes, ma'am." Energy coursed through him. He could hardly wait to do that job for Eva. He'd give her a hundred and ten percent, especially after all she'd paid.

"I now pronounce you bachelor and high bidder. May the contract between the two of you bring joy and satisfaction."

Had Deidre intended to echo the tone of wedding vows? He glanced at Eva, who looked uneasy, too.

Deidre cleared her throat. "As a designated representative of Raptors Rise, I want to thank you both for your support. As we like to say in Eagles Nest—*Your contribution is for the birds.*" She paused and looked up. "Okay, I know that's a lame joke, but my husband Jim thought of it and made me promise I'd use it this weekend. I'd like to tell him you laughed."

Nick managed a chuckle that sounded fake. Eva's was even worse, like she was gargling mouthwash. Eyebrows lifted, he met her gaze. She cracked up and so did he. Okay. They'd be fine.

6

In the salon, Eva was primarily in charge of her interaction with Nick. Sometimes he made suggestions about his haircut, but usually he put himself in her hands and let her tackle the job as she saw fit.

The dynamic had flipped tonight. She was in his world and he took the lead. Fine with her. She was somewhat in awe of him after that daredevil ride and still shaky from the adrenaline rush of the auction.

She and her friends had been such bachelor auction innocents. Ben Malone's dazzling display of horsemanship had been their first clue they were about to be blown away by a lineup of sexy cowboys. When Jared had barreled through those double doors, Beth had been toast.

She had done no better, losing all restraint when Nick had charged into the arena on a flashy palomino. She hadn't talked to Fiona yet, but quite likely she'd also burned through her limit to win Leo.

She didn't regret a thing. She'd had a blast competing for Nick and shutting out the wannabe bidders. Now she'd get her attic emptied, her rocks dug up, and maybe a waterfall built.

She'd also have fun partying with Nick tonight, and in this crowd, being with him was a plus. He had the respect and, in many cases, the love of the folks involved in the fundraiser. As the Winners' Circle filled with participants and supporters, he introduced her to those she hadn't met, mainly anyone who'd driven up from Eagles Nest.

CJ and Isabel were there, too. They'd booked appointments at the salon separately in the past couple of months, but Eva hadn't seen them together since Isabel had moved to Apple Grove. CJ clearly was besotted. He'd never looked at her the way he was looking at his fiancée.

To think she'd pegged him as a candidate for a casual fling—a carefree, guitar playing cowboy who'd keep it light and breezy. But this was the real CJ. Maybe she was slightly jealous of Isabel for snagging such a cutie-pie, but she wouldn't want to be in Isabel's boots, pregnant and planning her wedding.

When everyone headed up to Ed's house for what Ellie Mae called the *after-party*, Nick escorted her, his hand resting lightly against the small of her back. She'd touched him often during his hair appointments. Had he ever touched her?

Not on purpose. Her inclination to give clients a friendly pat on the shoulder didn't go both ways, did it? But Nick wasn't a client tonight and he'd underlined that fact with a gesture that signaled she was with him.

Ellie Mae led the procession as Ed's impressive house loomed ahead. Judging from the exterior, a combination of native stone and rough-hewn wood, it would live up to its reputation.

Ed had preceded them, and she opened the front door, a thick slab of carved wood. Rainbows of light spilled onto the porch from stained glass windows on either side of the door. They were shaped like a clover leaf with the initials EJV centered in each.

Nick pointed to them. "That's the outline of a barrel-racing course."

"Whoa. Subtle. I wouldn't have picked up on it."

Ellie Mae mounted the stone steps. "Edna Jane, you have done very well for yourself."

Ed laughed. "Thanks, Ellie Mae."

"When can I move in?"

"Anytime, Ellie Mae." Ed didn't bat an eye. "Happy to have you."

"Just kidding! I would never leave Eagles Nest. But I might be persuaded to visit you now and then."

"Your room will be waiting."

"Good. I'll make sure to check it out before I leave tonight." She took the final step to the porch and turned. "Get a move on, people! Time to par-tay!"

Eva followed the group up the steps and through the ginormous front door. Stepping aside to let others through, she paused to gape.

A massive rock fireplace with a gnarled wood mantle contrasted with glittering crystal chandeliers hanging from peeled-log beams.

Groupings of brightly colored furniture broke up the expanse of Ed's living room, inviting cozy chats. Western art decorated the walls.

"Nick, this is magnificent."

He leaned closer. "Wait until you taste the food."

"Looking forward to it." His comment made her smile. By the end of his first appointment, she'd figured out that eating was his favorite pastime.

No wonder he was excited about a party at Ed's. Food stations sat at convenient points around the room—fruit and cheese on one table, salads on one nearby, cold cuts on another, warm entrees in chafing dishes next to it and a dazzling array of desserts on yet another table. A bar was set up in a far corner.

She glanced up at Nick. "This must be your idea of heaven."

"Pretty much." He gestured to a coatrack by the door where several purses hung. "That's the official spot if you want to leave—"

"I do. Perfect." She looped the strap of hers over one of the empty hooks.

"Ready to dive in?"

"Absolutely. Lead the way." She made the rounds with him and ended up with more than she could eat because he insisted she try everything. Carrying full plates and crystal goblets of draft apple cider, they located a place to sit.

They were soon joined by Leo and Fiona. Before anyone had taken a bite, Ed showed up with a fancy camera.

"Hang on, boys! Don't start eating yet." She swept a hand toward the fireplace. "I need three minutes to get a group shot of all the bachelors right over there. I promise it won't take any longer than that."

After Nick and Leo put down their plates and excused themselves, Eva turned to Fiona. "Quick, I'm dying to know what you think of Leo."

"He's a perfect gentleman."

"And?"

She lowered her voice. "Guarded. He'd be tough to get to know."

"I certainly can't help you there, since I don't know him at all. I—" She paused as Beth came over holding her plate and a goblet of cider. "Hey, girlfriend." She motioned her to sit and leaned closer. "How's it going with Jared?"

"It's a work in progress. Evidently we don't know how to be together without talking about business."

"When's he taking you to the drive-in?"

"Tomorrow night."

She turned to Fiona. "When are you and Leo going—"

"Also tomorrow night."

"That settles it," Eva said. "Monday night we need to have dinner and compare notes."

Fiona nodded. "For sure. Come to my apartment at six. It's my turn to host."

"I'll be there," Eva said.

"Me, too." Beth glanced at them. "I couldn't hear how the bidding went. Did you guys stay within your budget?"

"I way overspent," Fiona said. "Same as you two."

"Eva, you blew your budget?" Beth stared at her. "I thought of all of us, you'd hold the line."

"I tried to stop her," Fiona said, "but it was a hopeless cause. Then I followed both of you down that rabbit hole. I won't be taking advantage of the Labor Day Weekend sales at Jeans Junction this year."

"Me, either," Eva said. "I blame the way they rode in."

"No kidding." Fiona pressed a hand to her heart. "Leo did this trick where he hung off one side of the saddle while the horse was galloping and then vaulted to the other side. I was so afraid he'd fall, but he was in complete control. I wonder if he was a stunt man before he moved here."

"Did you ask him?"

"Yes, and he dodged the question. I already know he doesn't want to discuss his past. He—"

"Zip it," Beth said. "The guys are coming back."

When Nick arrived, he took one look at Eva's goblet and held out his hand. "Looks like you need a refill."

Evidently during the conversation with Beth and Fiona, she'd drained her glass. Whoops. "Thank you, but please make it the virgin kind. I'm the designated driver."

"That reminds me," Fiona said. "Leo's offered to take me home."

"I'd planned to take Beth home, too." Jared turned to her. "That's if you want me to."

"I appreciate the offer, but I'll ride back with Eva."

"Oh," Fiona said. "Then so will I."

"That's silly." Eva didn't want to stand in the way of either of them spending time with their chosen guys. "I can—"

"I have a solution." Nick glanced down at her. "Let me drive you home and bring you back here in the morning to pick up your truck. I'll need to be at your house before eight, anyway, so I can get started on time. What do you say?"

"That's very gallant of you." From this angle his muscular chest was even more impressive. He'd taken her suggestion about wearing a tight T-shirt. Nice. "But then you can't enjoy an extra glass of cider."

He held her gaze. "Not a problem."

Had his eyes always been that blue? Maybe it was the navy T-shirt that emphasized the color. "Okay, then, thank you. A ride home would be lovely."

"Good." He smiled. "I'll fetch you a refill."

Ellie Mae's words came back to her. *You can count on this guy.* Nick had just removed responsibility from her shoulders so she could fully participate in this gala.

Why not let go of her duties for one evening? She loved her job and didn't mind the work involved with her house, but it might be time to relax and enjoy herself for a change.

7

Nick did his part to make a sizeable dent in the food but he switched to virgin cider for the rest of the evening. Small price to pay for being allowed to drive Eva home.

Even better, she was having a good time. No wonder. Ed knew how to throw a party. Or as Ellie Mae kept saying, an *after-party*.

Once everyone had a chance to eat their fill, Ed directed the Brotherhood to clear the furniture from the center of the room. The top-of-the-line sound system switched from background music to boisterous country tunes and the celebration kicked into high gear.

Line dancing was a favorite of the Babes, and turned out the Whine and Cheese ladies loved it, too. They started off with *Cotton-Eyed Joe* and Nick talked Eva into joining in.

Wouldn't you know they'd end up next to CJ and Isabel, who were great at it. Eva took one look at that couple and threw herself into the dance, her blue hair flying and her boots clicking on the wide-plank floor.

Alrighty, then. Nick's competitive streak kicked in, too, and he danced better than he had in his life. When the number ended, he grinned at Eva and held up his hand for a high-five.

Her breathless laughter warmed his heart as she smacked her palm against his.

"Nice job, bro." CJ punched him lightly on the arm. "You, too, Eva. Loved watching you guys."

"That was a blast." Breathing hard, Isabel placed a hand over her rounded tummy. "Cleo Marie is still dancing."

"Hey, folks!" Ellie Mae called out. "Don't go away! *Boot-Scootin' Boogie* is coming up!"

CJ looped an arm around Isabel's shoulders. "Are you and Cleo ready to take a break?"

"Heck, no. Let's do at least one more." She looked at Eva and Nick. "That's if you two are staying out here. Line dancing's more fun when you're next to people who really get into it."

Nick glanced at Eva. "You game?"

Her green eyes sparkled. "Sure."

"You have some great moves," Isabel said. "Ones I haven't seen before."

"Learned them from my Aunt Sally."

"Cool. You're very good."

"Thanks." She tilted her head in Nick's direction. "Have to keep up with this guy."

How he loved hearing the note of affection in her voice when she said that. The music started and he flashed her a smile as they lined up. Was she still stuck on CJ? Maybe, maybe not. Didn't matter. Tonight, she was with him. He planned to make the most of it.

Isabel was right about Eva's individuality on the dance floor. She had a snappy style that was all her own. Maintaining his rhythm was tough when he'd rather watch her shimmy in time to the music.

But line dancing was a group sport that required concentration and coordination. If he screwed up, he could impact her and potentially several others, including CJ and Isabel. That was unacceptable.

Good thing lifting weights had given him mental discipline. He could focus like nobody's business. Locked into the pattern, he was golden. He could have repeated it endlessly for... no telling how long.

The Brooks and Dunn tune only lasted for three minutes and eighteen seconds, though. He knew that because he lifted to country music and this was one of his favorites for a workout.

He was barely winded when the song was over, but Eva was gasping. He touched her shoulder. "Let's sit out the next one."

"Okay. Clearly I need to build up my stamina."

"We'll just have to do this more often, then." Maybe evenings at the Moose were in their future. He could dream. He turned to CJ. "We're taking a break."

"Good dancing with you and Eva, bro. We're heading home."

"Although I wish we could stay." Isabel sighed. "The party's just getting started, but now that I'm preggers, I can't hang in there like I used to."

"You're also putting a lot of effort into getting the coffee shop ready," Eva said. "Can't wait for it to open."

Isabel raised a fist. "Labor Day Weekend or bust!"

"You'll make it." CJ gave her a sideways hug and glanced at Nick and Eva. "You're both coming to the pre-opening night, I hope?"

"You know I will, bro." Depending on how tomorrow turned out, he might ask Eva if she'd like to go with him.

Eva nodded. "Wouldn't miss it. I—"

"Ladies and gentlemen, may I have your attention, please!" Ellie Mae moved to the center of the room. "I adore line dancing, but now and then I get nostalgic for a classic jitterbug. You may not know this, but Edna Jane rocks the jitterbug."

"Knock it off, Ellie Mae." Ed walked toward her. "These folks aren't into the jitterbug. They'd rather line dance or two-step or—"

"The question is, are *you* still into it?"

"Doesn't matter."

"I say it does. You've generously hosted this event and you loved to jitterbug back in the day."

"That doesn't mean I have to—"

"Why not? I trolled through your music collection and found the perfect tune—*Sold* by John Michael Montgomery. It's about falling in love during—"

"An auction." Ed sighed and gazed at Ellie Mae in obvious frustration. "I know."

"I cued it up. Come on, Edna Jane. Let's show the folks how a jitterbug is done."

"Nope. I'm not—"

She was drowned out by everyone chanting *Ed, Ed, Ed, Ed!*

"We're not leaving yet," CJ said.

Isabel laughed. "No way."

Ellie Mae signaled to Henri, who was positioned over by the sound system's control panel, and the music blasted out. Ellie Mae started to move with the beat and held her hand out to Ed.

"Oh, what the hell." Ed grinned and grabbed Ellie Mae's hand. She took the lead, twirling Ellie Mae in a dazzling display of jitterbug expertise. But Ellie Mae was no slouch. Everyone gasped when Ed slid Ellie Mae between her legs, but Ellie Mae popped right up and kept dancing.

A circle formed and everyone clapped in rhythm with the blistering pace of the tune and the dizzying motions of the two eighty-something dancers. Nick whistled through his teeth and got several answering whistles from the Brotherhood sprinkled throughout the crowd. The women ended the number with a dramatic double twirl and threw up their hands in triumph.

Nick cheered until he was hoarse. As the wave of applause slowed, he glanced down at Eva. "Was that amazing or what?"

"Incredible." She cleared her throat.

"It's been a long time since I've yelled like that."

"Me, too." She pulled a tissue from her pocket and dabbed at her eyes. "I wouldn't have missed it for the world." Her voice had a telltale quiver.

He moved closer. "Are you okay?"

"Yes. I just... they were so great." Her smile wobbled.

"I know." For some reason the performance by those two had grabbed her emotionally. He started to reach for her, then pulled back. Didn't want to overstep.

"The party has been wonderful." She took a deep breath. "But it's been a long week and I'm—"

"Ready to go home?"

"Yes, but you probably want to stay. CJ and Isabel haven't left yet. They can drop me off."

Like hell. He'd carry her home piggyback before he'd send her home in CJ's truck. "Leaving would be a good idea for me, too. I have barn duty at five."

Her eyes widened. "On top of giving me twelve hours of your time tomorrow?"

He shrugged. "Rafe and I volunteered so Matt, Jake and CJ can sleep in. Those three are handling everything else tomorrow so we can satisfy our auction obligations."

"Now that you mention it, I saw Rafe and Kate take off a little while ago, probably so he can get some sleep. If I'd wanted to stay late, would you have said anything?"

"Probably not."

"Because I bid so much money on you?"

"Not just that. I—" He caught himself before he said something incriminating. So far she hadn't figured out he was attracted to her. He'd like to keep it that way. "Well, mostly that, I guess."

"But—"

"Let's find Ed and thank her for the party. Then we'll vamoose."

She looked like she had more to say, but instead she nodded. "Okay." She gestured toward the crowd gathered around Ed and Ellie Mae. "Might not be all that easy to get to her."

"You could stay here and wait for me. I'll just work my way through—"

"I'll go with you. I want to rave about their dancing."

"Then grab hold of me." He held out his hand. "We're going in."

Her skin was soft but her grip was strong. Not surprising. When she massaged his scalp while shampooing his hair, her touch was firm. One more thing to like about her. He'd never gone for fragile women.

Being the guy who never asked for special favors paid off when you needed one. With a combination of smiles, apologies and gentle nudges, he maneuvered through the folks and cleared a path.

When they made it to the inner circle, Ellie Mae whooped with delight. "It's Eva of the blue hair! Edna Jane tells me you're a stylist. Do you have openings for a cut and color next week?"

Eva blinked. "I think I have Tuesday at three-thirty open, but I need to check. My phone's in my—"

"No worries. I'll call the salon and leave my number. You can let me know when you get a chance." She turned to Ed. "That's assuming I won't be abusing your hospitality if I stay through Tuesday."

"Nope. You can stay as long as you want."

"Not really. I'm needed in Eagles Nest. But I could wrangle a couple more days without causing a crisis at Pills and Pop." She glanced at Nick. "Don't think I ever told you how much I enjoyed your ride."

"Thank you, ma'am. I surely enjoyed that dance." He was still holding Eva's hand and she'd made no attempt to let go. Cozy.

"I *loved* your jitterbug." Eva zeroed in on Ed. "All this time you've been coming into the salon, and I had no idea you loved to jitterbug."

"First dance I ever learned."

"Same here. Watching you and Ellie Mae reminded me of... someone I miss."

Ed's expression softened. "Who's that, sweetheart?"

"My Aunt Sally."

"She was a dancer?"

"A great dancer until she was in a bad car accident."

"I didn't realize that. I wish I'd had a chance to know her." She reached over and touched Eva's arm.

"Me, too. If she'd been more comfortable traveling... but from Helena to here would have been too hard on her. Anyway, I wanted to tell you how much I loved the party. And your jitterbug. But I'm starting to fade, so Nick's offered to take me home."

"Well, thanks for coming." Ed beamed at her. "And for your contribution to the cause."

"My pleasure." She turned to Ellie Mae. "I'll look forward to hearing from you." "She squeezed Nick's hand and let go. "We're off."

"Thanks for a great party." Nick gave Ed a quick smile before turning and following Eva back through the crowd.

As they made their way to the coat rack to fetch Eva's purse, he was intercepted by several folks wanting to comment on his ride. Took longer than he'd planned to get going.

Eventually they slipped out the door and started down the steps. "Sorry about that."

"No apology necessary. You were great."

"Thanks. I forgot to mention that I'm parked all the way down by the arena."

"I don't mind the walk. Is the palomino you rode yours?"

"Ed's horse. Name's Thor."

"He's beautiful. Do you have a horse of your own?"

"No, ma'am. Thought about it many times, but there's no shortage of good horses to ride at the Buckskin and the upkeep on one is expensive. I'd rather see my savings grow."

"That's very sensible. What are you saving for?"

"A place of my own."

"You'd leave the ranch?"

"Wouldn't have to. Henri's recently announced that any of us who'd like our own house can build it on her land. CJ will be the third one to take advantage of that."

"Do you have a spot in mind?"

"Not yet." He didn't plan to start until he could build the house without going into debt. But he hesitated to mention that to Eva, who'd just taken on a big mortgage.

He switched topics. "When did your Aunt Sally teach you to jitterbug?"

"Soon after I moved in with her, so I'm guessing I was around three."

"That's young." Something must have happened with her parents, then.

"She loved to dance, and she started training me early so I could be her partner, which was great fun for me. By the time I was eight I could do all the major dances—waltz, tango, foxtrot, mambo, you name it."

"Makes sense those two ladies stirred memories of her."

"She'd have fit right in. Or she would have if she hadn't been in a car accident. She was a hale and hearty seventy-four when that happened."

"Seventy-four? Your aunt?"

"Great-aunt."

"You said something about the trip from Helena. If she was there, how'd you end up here?"

"When she had to go into assisted living, I enrolled in a beauty academy in Great Falls and met Josette. She heard about a salon for sale in Apple Grove so we bought it. And for years I made weekly trips to Helena to visit Aunt Sally."

Might be another reason he hadn't seen her around town. "It sounds like your Aunt Sally was a terrific woman."

"The best."

A good place to leave the discussion. But he'd like to know more. It sounded as if she'd lost her only relative when her great aunt died. That was tough. She might not want to discuss the ramifications of being without any kin, but if she ever did, he was an expert on the subject.

8

Aunt Sally had deserved a better end than she'd had, and it used to hurt a lot to talk about her. But Eva had started to heal. Two years ago, watching those ladies jitterbugging their hearts out, would have turned her into a faucet.

Nick handed her into his spotless silver truck like the gentleman he was. She thanked him and settled into the seat. Most of the cowboys she'd met took pride in their trucks, even if they had a lot of miles on them. Nick was no exception.

He climbed behind the wheel, buckled up and started the engine. A country tune on high volume poured from the speakers. He switched it off.

"You can leave the music on if you want."

"Okay, but that was way too loud." He adjusted the volume. "I blasted it on the way over because I was so nervous."

"It didn't show."

"Riding fast helped some." He backed the truck around and drove across the dirt yard to the paved road leading to the highway. "Windows down or up?"

"Let's put them down, please. It's a nice night." As the previous song ended, Keith Whitley's *When You Say Nothing at All* spilled gently from the speakers. She cranked her window down and so did he. This truck was an old-timer.

The moon rode low on the horizon and a warm breeze drifted through the open window. Crickets chirped from the roadside. She glanced over at Nick, his hands resting loosely on the wheel, his broad shoulders relaxed.

She appreciated his willingness to let the silence between them just be, filled only with the gentle tones of the song. His calm, supportive mood surrounded her like a soft blanket.

He'd been a considerate friend, coaxing her to enjoy the party and facilitating that by offering her a ride home. He'd almost hugged her tonight when he'd noticed she was upset. She wouldn't have minded. She'd bet he was a good hugger.

The Keith Whitley song ended and a commercial came on. She turned to Nick. "I've been thinking about your schedule tomorrow. Since you have barn duty at five, why don't you come to my house later in the morning, like ten or eleven?"

"That would mean I'd be there later, too, but if you'd rather follow that schedule, I could—"

"You don't have to stay until ten at night. You could still leave at eight."

He gave her a quick glance. "That's not what you paid for."

"Doesn't matter."

"It does to me." He returned his attention to the deserted road. "I offered twelve hours of manual labor and that's what I'll deliver." He chuckled. "You don't want to mess with that contract we both agreed to. Deidre will come after us."

"She might. That sounded like a binding agreement."

"Sure did."

"Do you know what she does for a living? My guess is she's a lawyer."

"Don't quote me on this, but I think she's a real estate agent."

"That would fit, too. Anyway, regarding our *contract*, I think it puts me in the power position."

"It does. I'm yours to command."

There was that sexy bachelor auction vibe Fiona had talked about. It put sizzle into this conversation. "In that case, I should be free to cut your hours." The atmosphere in the truck's cab had shifted to a teasing one and she was fine with that.

"Why would you want me to work less? Last time I heard, you had several things on your list."

"I didn't know you were getting up at five for barn duty. Besides, you're giving me a ride home and you're planning to give me another ride back to fetch my truck. That takes up any slack."

"Not in my book. Unless you forbid me to start work at eight, that's when I'll begin. I want you to get your money's worth."

"I made a charitable donation to a cause I care about. Even if you didn't do a lick of work, I'd still—"

"Did you just find a chest full of money in that attic?"

"No."

"You told me on Wednesday that you probably couldn't afford whatever I'd bring at this auction. At the time, I had no idea the bidding would go so high. Or that you'd hang in there. Judging from what you said during my hair appointment, you can't have planned to spend—"

"I didn't."

"Then why'd you do it? I tried to warn you off. Did you see me shaking my head?"

"I saw you."

"Why didn't you back off?"

Because you rode in on a fast horse to a song I happen to love and I couldn't help myself. She was a sucker for a man with flair. Nick had surprised her by being dashing. She wasn't ready to say that. "Zane McGavin's opening speech."

"I couldn't hear it."

"It was very inspiring. I couldn't resist donating to such a worthwhile cause, but to do that I had to win the bid. Which I did."

"And you no longer care whether you get stuff down from the attic or rocks out of your yard?"

"Well, I do, but not if you're working yourself to the bone."

"Working myself to the bone is what I do. It's my thing."

"You're just saying that to make me feel better."

"Trust me, I'm not. I'm never happier than when I have a physically demanding job ahead of me." He pulled up in front of her Victorian and switched off the engine.

"I don't buy that *never happier* stuff. I'm sure there are several things you like even better."

"Like what?"

"For one thing, a plate full of delicious food."

He laughed.

"I was there, Nick. I saw your reaction to Ed's buffet."

"Let's say good food and a physical challenge are equally appealing. And they complement each other. Working hard makes me hungry and eating well gives me fuel for the tough jobs." He opened his door and grabbed his hat off the dash. "I'll walk you to the porch."

"You don't have to."

"Yes, I do. Wait for me, please."

She did. She even waited for him to open the door and help her down. She got a kick out of his take charge attitude in the short term. In the long term, it might start to chafe.

Her front walk was wide and should accommodate two, although tonight was the first time she'd tested that. When one of the people was Nick, it was a close fit. He jostled her shoulder and apologized.

"No worries. I don't break."

"I recognize that about you."

"Even though I get teary-eyed when two eighty-something women dance the jitterbug?"

"Everybody has a soft spot for something."

"What's yours?"

"Baby animals. Foals, kittens, puppies, tiny cottontails, bear cubs, you name it. I get choked up."

"Children, too?"

"Aw, yeah. Those little shavers when they first learn to walk. So cute and brave."

"So I'm all about the older folks and you're all about the kids." She climbed her porch steps and he followed her up.

"Those two groups are alike, in a way."

She turned to face him. "How so?"

"They both have gumption."

"I guess they do. Never thought of that." She dug out her keys. "Getting back to what you said about fuel for tough jobs, if I can't change your mind about the hours you work tomorrow, I can cook for you."

"Oh, that's not necess—"

"Hey, I'm going along with your plan of twelve hours, so you can jolly well go along with mine." She lifted her chin, ready to take a stand. His hat shaded his face from the muted glow of the porch light and partially disguised his expression. "You love to eat and I love feeding people. I'll cook for you or know the reason why."

He nudged his hat back. The soft light reflected in his blue eyes, making them sparkle. He smiled. "I'd be a fool to pass up that offer."

Her breath caught. Nick Le Grande was a *very* handsome guy. How had she missed that? As she held his gaze, the blue of his eyes deepened to navy. Her stomach fluttered.

Then he swallowed, touched two fingers to the brim of his hat and backed away. "See you at seven-thirty, Eva."

"Seven-thirty? I thought eight was the—"

"I need to drive you back to Ed's to get your truck, and I do plan to start at eight."

"Oh, right." What was up with her breathing? "Seven-thirty it is, then."

He took the porch steps two at a time and lengthened his stride when he reached the sidewalk.

The growl of his truck's engine and the flash of headlights snapped her out of her daze. Spinning around, she opened the screen door and jabbed the key in the lock. Took two tries to get the door open.

Once inside, she laid her purse and keys on the side table by the door and stood in the entryway dragging in air. They'd been talking about oldsters and puppies, and then...

What had just happened?

9

Extra sleep. Yeah, right. Nick was up, dressed and slugging down coffee by the time Rafe, his barn-duty partner, stumbled into the darkened kitchen buttoning his shirt.

"You could turn on a light, y'know," he muttered.

"Don't need it."

"Whatcha doing up so early?"

"Couldn't sleep."

"Eva?"

"Yep."

"Figured." Rafe took a mug from the cupboard, forgot to close the door and banged his head. He swore softly.

"Want me to turn on a light?"

"Not *now*. Damage is done." He handed Nick the mug. "I'd appreciate it if you'd pour it for me, seeing as how you have night vision. I'm liable to scald myself."

Nick grinned. "I'll turn on a—"

"Heck, no. You'll spoil all the fun of pretending we're living in olden times."

"Sarcasm doesn't become you." He handed Rafe a steaming mug.

"I'd say it fits me perfectly. I take it you're jacked up about spending the day at Eva's place?"

"Keep your voice down."

"No worries. Those boys are nighty-night. Anyway, we all know you're hung up on her. Stands to reason you'd be anticipating today's assignment like a kid on Christmas morning."

"I'm not that far gone." He was exactly that far gone. "Here's the thing. Last night, when we were saying goodbye on her porch, there was a moment when I'd swear she was into me."

"Don't go kidding yourself. I've made that mistake too many times with Kate."

"I don't think I'm wrong, but speaking of Kate, aren't you taking her out for a day-long horseback ride in a few hours?"

"That I am. I knew she planned on bidding to win, but I don't think she can afford what she ended up paying."

"Same with Eva."

"I thought about offering to reimburse Kate, but she'd just get mad. I'll make the ride as nice as I can. Jake's fixing a lunch for us."

"Have you ever been alone with Kate?"

"Not to this extent. Jake thinks I should make a move, but..."

"You should."

"I will if you will."

"Forget it, bro. Our situations are totally different. You and Kate have been dancing around each other for almost two years. I've only known Eva since March, and until two months ago she was all about CJ."

"Who's now happily engaged, so you have a clear shot."

"I'm not saying I'll never make a move, but it won't be today. Like you pointed out, I could be wrong about that look she gave me last night."

"Can you describe it?"

Nick sipped his coffee. "She was on a rant about how if I insisted on giving her twelve hours of hard labor, she'd by God cook me a bunch of food in return. I was planning to take my own, but she'd worked up a head of steam about providing it for me."

"That's a good sign. Women don't tend to cook for a guy unless they like him."

"I thought it was great that she wanted to, so I gave her a big smile and accepted her offer. That's when she stared at me like she was seeing me for the first time."

"Maybe you had food in your teeth."

"I didn't. I checked later."

"A booger in your nose?"

"No, Rafe. Not a *booger*. I think she felt something."

"Likely heartburn, then. Lots of rich food last night. Those crackers topped with cheese and jalapeno would give anybody—"

"Damn it, that's not what I was getting from her. I'd know if it was indigestion. In that moment, she was into me. Startled us both."

"For your sake, I hope you're right." Rafe rinsed his mug in the sink and put it in the dishwasher. "Ready to go feed those ponies? Leo's up, too. He said he'd be down in a few minutes. That way we'll get done faster."

"Good." Nick gulped the last of his coffee, rinsed his mug and put it in the dishwasher rack next to Rafe's. *Had* he misinterpreted Eva's expression last night? What if she'd suddenly remembered she'd left her curling iron turned on? Or a candle burning?

That made no sense, though. If she'd remembered something like that, she would have quickly excused herself and rushed inside. Instead she'd stayed right where he'd left her, like her boots were nailed to the porch.

Then again, she'd been emotional after watching Ellie Mae and Ed jitterbug. He'd be wise not to expect a similar response from her in the light of a new day. At least he'd be allowed to spend more time with her than he ever had before.

Her offer to prepare some food had promise according to Rafe. She wouldn't bring him a plate and leave him to eat it alone, either. That wasn't Eva. They'd eat at least one meal together. Likely two.

Barn duty went quickly with three of them working, so Nick left Leo and Rafe to finish up. Hot-footing it to the bunkhouse, he cleaned up before helping Garrett fix breakfast. Garrett had taken over kitchen detail except for chuck-wagon stew night on Friday. That was still Jake's deal.

Nick usually made toast, leaving the eggs and bacon to Garrett. That cowboy had a way with scrambled eggs, always finding new ingredients to throw into the pan.

This morning he wanted to add red peppers and mushrooms and Nick offered to chop them for him. Used to be CJ's job. He'd taught Nick a few of his techniques.

Garrett hummed under his breath as he laid strips of bacon onto the cast-iron griddle. Humming wasn't typical for the Buckskin's newest hire.

Nick glanced at him. "Have fun last night?"

"I did, actually. Darcy loves being a vet and can't wait to start helping with the raptors. First time I've had a chance to talk to her."

"First time I've laid eyes on her, let alone had a conversation. Sounds like you enjoyed her company."

"Yep."

"We're here," Rafe called out as he and Leo came through the front door. "Do we have time for a shower?"

"If you make it snappy!" Garrett hollered back.

Nick finished his chopping and moved into toast-making mode. "What are you doing with Darcy for your auction thing? I can't remember."

"We're heading up to Glacier today for lunch and sightseeing."

"Any sparks between you two?"

Garrett smiled. "No. We even tested that with a kiss last night. Zero chemistry. We had a good laugh about it, which tells me we're going to be great friends. That's fine, too."

"Good way to look at it." Could he take that attitude with Eva? Didn't seem likely. He had sparks flying everywhere. "I guess I just assumed since she bid on you, she was interested."

"She was willing to entertain the possibility. So was I. Like I said—no chemistry. But Raptors Rise benefitted and we both want to see Glacier. It's all good."

"I admire how you roll with the punches."

"Had plenty of practice." He looked over at the toaster. "Better get that toast buttered quick. We're ready."

"And so am I, gents." Leo walked into the kitchen, his hair still damp from the shower. "After all I ate last night, I thought I'd never be hungry again, but one whiff of frying bacon and my stomach's talking to me."

Nick piled toast on a platter and set it on the table. "Grab a plate. I made a fresh pot of coffee."

"Take an apple, too," Garrett said. "Nobody eats enough fruit around here. I buy it and it just sits there."

Leo grinned and plucked an apple from a bowl on the counter. "Yes, Mom." Then he turned toward the doorway. "Think fast, bro!" He tossed the apple at Rafe as he came down the aisle between the bunks.

Rafe caught it in one large hand. "What am I supposed to do with this?"

"Eat it. It's good for you." Leo picked up another apple. "Here you go, Nick." He lobbed it over. "Garrett, you, too." He placed an apple near the stove and snatched the last one from the bowl before looking over at Garrett. "Happy, now?" He took a large bite.

Garrett rolled his eyes. "Delirious."

Rafe finished his in no time. "That's enough standing around eating apples." He took a plate from the stack on the counter and filled it from the food simmering on the stove. "I have places to go and things to do."

"We can tell," Leo said. "You put on half a bottle of cologne."

"Don't tease him," Nick said. "He's already nervous."

"Am not." Rafe pulled out a chair and sat.

"Well, I am." Nick piled food on his plate and carried it to the table. "This is my big chance with Eva and I'm scared I'll blow it."

"I notice it doesn't affect your appetite," Leo said.

"Nothing affects my appetite." He went for coffee before sitting down. Then it hit him. Out of habit, he'd loaded his plate like he usually did. But his gut was tight with anxiety. He had absolutely no interest in taking even a single bite.

But he'd eat it all, stuff it down if necessary. For one thing, he'd just announced that nothing spoiled his appetite. For another, and this was more important than saving face, wasting food drove him crazy.

<u>10</u>

When Nick parked in front of her house, Eva pulled the cinnamon rolls out of the oven and left them on the counter to cool. If he'd had barn duty this morning and yet had committed to showing up here at seven-thirty he'd likely left the bunkhouse without much more than a cup of coffee.

Even if he'd had breakfast, he wouldn't have had time to eat much. Nick loved his food. She'd make sure he started the day off right. They could eat first and fetch her truck afterward.

She'd set two places at the kitchen table, had a breakfast casserole keeping warm in the oven and a festive bowl of sliced bananas, strawberries and kiwi ready to go. The Apple Grove Market occasionally surprised her with delicacies like kiwi. She'd splurged and bought some this week.

She'd made Brazilian coffee from freshly-ground beans and poured it into a thermal carafe. She had half-and-half in the fridge, although most cowboys she'd met took it black.

When he rang her doorbell, she surveyed her preparations one last time and walked to the front door, adrenaline pouring through her system. She'd dreamed about him last night, dreams that made her blush.

Seeing him in person should help. It was just Nick. That moment on the porch had been the result of an emotionally charged evening. She blamed the dream on too much rich food.

Taking a calming breath, she unlocked the door and pulled it open. Damn. He looked even better this morning.

Hat in hand, feet braced apart, he stood on the other side of her screen door, filling the space with his wide shoulders. His snowy white T-shirt, nearly as snug as the navy one, emphasized the breadth of his muscular chest. He exuded physical power, as if he could handle anything.

Might as well admit that he turned her on. But she didn't have to let him know. "Good morning."

"Morning, ma'am. Ready to go get your truck?"

"Not yet." She unlatched the screen and pushed it open. "Come in. I want to feed you a proper breakfast before we leave."

"Breakfast?" He frowned. "Oh, no, ma'am. I don't need—"

"We had an agreement, remember?" She breathed in the tantalizing scent of soap, cologne and healthy male. "Whatever you grabbed on the way out the door couldn't possibly be enough to get you through a morning of lugging stuff from the attic and digging up rocks. Everything's ready and the cinnamon rolls should be cooled by now."

"Cinnamon rolls?" He stepped inside.

For some reason his expression hadn't brightened. Was it possible he didn't care for them? "Maybe you're not a fan."

"Oh, I love cinnamon rolls. I just hate to think of you going to so much trouble."

"Making them is fun for me—kneading the dough, shaping the rolls, the wonderful smell while they're baking."

"I thought you were burning one of those scented candles."

"Those don't smell as good as the real thing. And not to brag, but I make a killer cinnamon roll." She left the front door open to allow cool morning air to drift through the screen.

The oven had heated up the place. Add in the presence of a big strong cowboy and the breeze was mighty welcome. "I've set us up in the kitchen."

"You haven't had breakfast, either?" He followed her in.

"No."

"Well, then." He cleared his throat. "Mighty nice of you to include me."

"I figured why not? I love cooking and you love eating. Have a seat."

"Not until you do."

She glanced at his mannerly and extremely sexy self. Whew. "Then let me take the casserole out of the oven and bring over the rolls. Then we can—"

"You made a casserole, too?"

"Don't worry. It's easy-peasy. The cinnamon rolls take effort. The casserole only involves throwing the ingredients together." She grabbed oven mitts, pulled the baking dish from the oven and set it on the trivets she'd put on the table earlier.

"Smells great."

"Doesn't it? Pairing this with cinnamon rolls might be a little heavy under normal circumstances, but you have intensely physical work ahead of you. This meal will help get you through the morning."

"Looks substantial." He took a quick breath. "And smells delicious. Ready to sit?"

"Let's see... I think that's it. Wait, do you use anything in your coffee?"

"No, ma'am."

"Ha. Nailed it. Then yes, I'm ready to sit." She gestured to her place. "This one."

He pulled out her chair. "You must have been up early to do all this."

"I was, but cooking is more rewarding when you're sharing the meal with someone." She slipped into the chair he held for her. She'd been this close to him many times in the salon without hyperventilating. Maybe the cape had shielded her from his tasty pheromones.

"Well, I surely appreciate it." He took the spot she'd set for him, catty-corner from her. He hung his hat on the back of the chair nearest to him.

"Let me have your plate. I'll dish you some casserole. Do you like fruit?"

"I... ah... sure."

"Ever had kiwi?"

"Must be the green one with the little black seeds. No, I haven't."

"You'll love it. Comes from New Zealand. Doesn't show up that often in the market here, but it did this past week." She gave him a large helping of casserole and two heaping spoons of fruit salad. Then she paused. "One cinnamon roll or two?"

"One is fine."

"You're just being polite. I'll only eat one of these. You can have the other five."

"I would never take more than my share."

"Please don't hold back on my account. They're best when they're fresh. When I make them for myself, they go stale before I can finish them. Unlike you, I don't have a huge appetite."

"Must drive you nuts when you have them go stale."

"Believe me, it does. I want these eaten ASAP. I'll leave the dish on the counter so you can help yourself to any you don't eat now."

"I..." His breath hitched. "That's very generous."

"Sure you don't want two?"

"Just one, thanks. If I'm going to start at eight, we need to go fetch your truck soon."

"I guess that start time really is important to you." She dished herself.

"The sooner I start, the sooner I'll be out of your way. I intend to give you twelve hours, one way or another."

"I can't gauge how long either of these jobs will take. Maybe you'll have all the stuff out of the attic by ten, which leaves you a whole bunch of time to dig up the rocks. If you're as efficient as Rafe says, that won't take long, either." She ate a bite of the casserole because clearly he was waiting for her to start.

He dug into his, popped a forkful into his mouth, chewed and swallowed. "Very good. Excellent."

"Thanks."

He forked up another bite. "Is there anything else you'd like me to do if I finish early? I'll bet you could come up with something." He'd said it straight-faced, without a wink or a knowing smile.

Clearly last night's moment on the porch hadn't translated to flirting today. "I probably could. It's an old house."

"And a big house. How many rooms?"

"Eight if you count the attic, nine if you count the enclosed back porch. Three bedrooms and a bathroom upstairs, kitchen, living room and dining room downstairs. Eventually I'll add another bathroom when I can afford it."

"Any dripping faucets or leaking pipes? Old plumbing can be dicey."

"Why? Do you have a plumber's license?"

He smiled at that. "No."

There was that great smile again. Made her catch her breath.

"That said, I'm fairly handy." He speared a slice of kiwi. "Working on a guest ranch, especially one that's been around a while, you learn things out of necessity. Henri and Charley taught us basic skills so we could deal with minor repairs in the guest cabins."

"In that case, I'm sure I can come up with enough things to keep you busy. Of course we'll be taking time out for lunch and dinner. I insist on that." She picked up her cinnamon roll. "How do you like the kiwi?"

"It's good. Glad I got to try it. But you know, after this wonderful and filling breakfast, I won't need any lunch." He tucked back into his casserole.

"I don't believe that for a minute. While you're bringing things down from the attic, I'll put together a pot of chili. I like making cornbread to go with it. I usually top the chili with cheese. Do you like it that way?"

"I do, but seriously, why not save the chili for dinner and skip lunch? This is a big breakfast, and if I'm going to be snacking on cinnamon rolls all day, then—"

"Are you worried that I'm putting too much effort into feeding you?"

"Yes, ma'am. That's it, exactly."

"Then you can help me make dinner."

"Of course I'd be glad to help."

Judging from his expression, he wasn't entirely happy with the meal program she'd laid out. Made sense. Just because he loved to eat didn't mean he was comfortable having her spend extra time in the kitchen. And it was a hot day.

She shifted her plan from a roast in the oven to steaks on the grill. "Tell you what. We'll cook out tonight—grill steaks and corn, roast the potatoes in the coals. Oh, and I have pie from the Apple Barrel for dessert. With ice cream."

"Sounds great." He paused, the cinnamon roll halfway to his mouth. "But it sure is a lot of food."

"Maybe for some people, but not you. You're famous for your appetite."

He gave her another of those great smiles. "Yes, ma'am. That's a fact." And he bit into the roll.

11

Nick managed not to groan as he followed Eva up the narrow stairs to the attic. Against his better judgment, he'd eaten a second cinnamon roll because she'd looked disappointed when he'd stopped with one. Rafe had said a woman didn't cook for a guy unless she liked him.

If Rafe was right, then Eva liked him a whole lot. And he risked derailing her positive feelings if he skimped on the food she'd worked so hard to make.

When she'd offered another helping of casserole, he'd taken it, too. Her cheeks had glowed pink with pleasure when he'd raved about the meal. Worth a little pain, right?

Scratch that. A *lot* of pain. His stomach had ached in silent protest during the drive out to Ed's place. Coming back, he'd been by himself and he'd loosened his belt a couple of notches.

But the mark from his typical cinching showed on the leather. Vanity had made him tighten the belt again before leaving the truck.

He'd never been so stuffed in his life. But the food wasn't the only culprit. Under normal circumstances he might have handled two heavy meals in a row. These weren't normal circumstances.

For the first time, he was completely alone with Eva. Judging from her cooking frenzy, she was warming to him. That suggested possibilities that stole his breath and tightened his gut. His very full gut.

Ahead of him on the stairs, she lovingly described the many idiosyncrasies of the house. He managed some appropriate responses and studied the worn tread beneath his boots to avoid looking at the sweet curve of her backside as she climbed.

He had a slight tendency toward impatience that could tank the whole program. Just because he had the opportunity to initiate something didn't mean he should.

The day was young. He'd give them both time to get used to each other. Let things happen naturally.

"These stairs creak a lot more than the ones between the first and second floor." She reached the top of the stairs and opened a rustic wooden door.

"Is that something you'd like me to work on?"

"Not really. Creaking stairs don't bother me. Aunt Sally used to say it was the house talking to her."

"She had a house like this?" That could explain a lot.

"Very similar." She walked into the attic. "Watch your head when you come through the doorway."

"Thanks." He ducked, stepped over a sill and into the musty attic. At least somebody had laid down a floor. He straightened and glanced around. A low-wattage bulb hanging from the rafters gave off enough weak light to get a vague idea of what was up here.

An oval full-length mirror stood in a far corner next to a carved wooden coat tree hung with a pink feather boa. Cardboard boxes and wooden chests were piled within the circle of light. Could be more in the shadows.

To his right sat the most visible item in the attic and the only one without a speck of dust. What little light there was gleamed on the lustrous black surface of a large leather trunk with a curved lid.

He pointed to it. "Looks like something out of a movie."

"Doesn't it? It might be too big for one person. I could take an end so we can get it downstairs."

"I can handle it." He walked over, grasped the leather handles on either end and lifted it a few inches off the floor. No heavier than a bale of hay. "Piece of cake. What's in it?"

"I don't know. It's locked. I've found a few keys in a drawer but none of them fit. If you can haul it to the first floor, I'll call a locksmith tomorrow."

Crouching down, he examined the old-fashioned keyhole. "I could probably open it."

"Yeah?"

"I think so."

"Is that something Henri and Charley taught you, too?"

"No, ma'am. I perfected that skill a long time ago." It had come in handy when he'd had to live by his wits.

She gazed at him. "Sounds like there's a story there."

"Not a very interesting one." Petty theft, a stint in juvie—he'd rather keep those tales to himself. "Want me to start with this trunk, then?"

"I'd love that, especially if you can get it open."

"Let's do it." He hefted the trunk, eager to be the hero who worked some magic with his pocket knife. He turned sideways so he could get the trunk through the narrow door.

How cool it would be to throw back the lid and solve the mystery of what had been locked away, maybe for years. Eva would be so grateful for—*bam*. Smacking the side of his head on the doorframe wasn't part of the plan.

"Nick!"

"No worries." Ears ringing, he ducked the way he should have in the first place and started down the stairs. His head throbbed enough to block the ache in his stomach. Bonus.

She followed him. "Stop when you get to the second floor. I want to evaluate the damage to your head."

"It's nothing." He'd learned his lesson, though. He used extra caution navigating the narrow stairway. Missing a step would be bad news for him, the creaky wood beneath his boots and this precious trunk.

"Didn't sound like nothing. Sounded like you whacked it good."

"I have a hard head." Or so he'd been told each time he'd landed in the ER after a fight back in the day.

"I insist you let me check it out. My first-aid supplies are in my bathroom on the second floor. That's the most convenient spot to assess the situation. Stop there."

"Yes, ma'am." She was the boss on this job. She'd paid for the privilege of telling him what to do. He arrived at the landing. "Where do you want me?"

"Set the trunk down, first."

He did as he was told and turned to her as she descended the last few steps.

Walking over, she reached for his chin and gently turned it so she could see the right side of his head. "You didn't break the skin but it's swelling."

"I'm not worried about it."

An impatient snort was followed by an eye roll. "Come into the bathroom. I'll put some cream on it to start and get you an ice pack when we go down to the first floor."

"The cream's okay but an ice pack will slow me down." He followed her in and was instantly surrounded by the fragrance she used, one that smelled like sunshine and flowers.

"You don't have to hold it on there for long. Even ten minutes will help a lot."

"I don't need—"

"Shh." She gestured to the closed lid of the toilet. "Sit there."

"I never realized you were so bossy."

"I never realized you were so stubborn." She opened a drawer, grabbed a tube and twisted off the cap.

"What is it?"

"A magical potion that makes you putty in my hands."

Already there. "Seriously, what is—"

"Arnica. Helps with pain and reduces bruising and swelling."

"That should be enough then. I don't need an ice pack."

"Yes, you do. Now hold still." She moved in close, leaning toward him the way she did when she was shampooing his hair.

As she smoothed the cream over the tender spot at his temple, her breasts hovered inches from his face. Their gentle movement as she breathed sent his pulse rate skyrocketing. He gripped his knees and closed his eyes.

"Does that hurt?"

"No, ma'am."

"Does, too. You're clenching your jaw."

Not the reason. He loosened his jaw muscles.

"That should do it." As she moved away, the warm air pocketed between them shifted.

He kept a tight hold on his knees. He was dangerously close to reaching for her. Gradually opening his eyes, he met the concern reflected in hers. He swallowed. "Thanks."

"Promise you'll watch out for that low-hanging doorframe from now on."

"I promise." *Need any more promises, Eva? I have a bucketful of them. Just give me the word.*

_12_

Eva hadn't mistaken the look in Nick's eyes this time. His gaze darkened the way it had last night and his breathing changed. If she leaned down and kissed him, he'd be okay with that.

Boy, was she tempted. His heart-stopping ride into the arena had placed him in hot cowboy territory and he'd only added to his appeal since then. His lips parted slightly as if he might be reading her thoughts, gauging what she'd do next.

Awareness hummed through her veins. The prospect of being tucked against his firm body tightened her nipples and sent warmth rushing to her lady parts.

Just in time, she grasped a lifeline of self-preservation and backed away. She didn't know his expectations and he had no clue about hers. That was how people got hurt and she had no desire to hurt Nick. She liked him too much.

She broke eye contact and put the top back on the arnica tube. "Stay here and I'll go get the ice pack."

He stood. "The trunk's halfway there and the next set of stairs is easier." A husky note in his voice sent a shiver up her spine.

"And once it's delivered to the first floor, you'll relax for ten minutes with an ice pack?"

"Yes, ma'am."

"Alrighty, then." She left the bathroom and waited while he regained his hold on the trunk. Then she followed him down. Better keep an eye on him and look for signs of disorientation since he'd sustained a head injury.

He seemed fine. Mighty fine. His tight shirt revealed the smooth ripple of his shoulder and back muscles as he maneuvered the trunk around the curve of the staircase. Snug jeans helped her determine that his quads and glutes worked perfectly, too.

Nick had turned out to be eye-candy, just as her friends had predicted. Even though he'd sat in her chair at the salon multiple times, she'd been blind to his attributes, maybe because she'd been focused on CJ.

Musicians make perfect lovers. Aunt Sally had said that dozens of times. They have rhythm and style. Even better, if they're good enough, they go on tour, giving you days, weeks, months of time to do your own thing.

Her aunt's recommendation had been reinforced every time she'd treated them both to another country music event. Invariably, Eva had picked the blond performers as her favorites. She'd developed a type and CJ had fit that type.

Nick did not. But tell that to her damp panties.

He neared the bottom step. "Where to?"

"The living room, please. I dusted the bottom, too, so you can put it on the rug."

"Got it."

"While you're icing your head, I'm going to have you sit in one of the wingbacks. They're roomie."

He chuckled. "Are you implying I'm too large for the rest of your living room furniture?"

"I want you to be comfortable."

"Appreciate it." He walked into the living room, set down the trunk on the area rug and glanced around. "This is nice. But you're right to put me in one of the wingbacks. I might break that loveseat. Or get permanently wedged in one of those side chairs."

"The furniture's stronger than it looks, but it wasn't built with you in mind. Have a seat while I get the ice pack."

"I'd like to look around, instead."

"Okay. I'll be right back." She hurried into the kitchen.

"These lampshades are amazing," he called out.

"The Tiffany ones?" She pulled a gel ice pack out of the freezer and wrapped it in a kitchen towel.

"The ones made of stained glass. I don't know what they're called."

"That's a Tiffany-style." She walked into the living room where he was examining one of the floor lamps. "I'm not sure if they're authentic or a knockoff, but I don't care. I leave them on, even in the daylight, because they're so beautiful when they're lit."

"That seems like the whole point, to have light shining through them."

"That's what I think." She handed him the towel-wrapped gel pack.

"Thank you." He pressed it gingerly against his temple.

"How does it feel?"

He grinned. "Cold. Very cold."

"Smart-aleck." She gestured to the nearest wingback. "It'll probably work better if you sit down and relax."

"I'm fine." He remained standing and continued to survey the room. "I like that picture that's hanging over the loveseat. Did it come with the house?"

"No. It's mine." She could demand that he sit down, but maybe it didn't matter that much. "It was Aunt Sally's favorite, one of the few things she kept out of the estate sale. Assisted living is expensive. She needed the cash."

"The woman in the picture looks so happy."

"That's why Aunt Sally loved it. She said it symbolizes the joys of freedom."

"Freedom from what?"

She hesitated. He'd asked the right question. Should she get into it? Then again, she'd almost kissed him a few minutes ago. Yeah, she should get into it.

"What the other people in her life expected of her. When a doctor told her she was unlikely to have kids, she ditched the concept of marriage, too. "

"Not everyone is cut out for it."

"Her family couldn't accept that. She was supposed to get married and drive herself crazy trying to give her parents grandchildren. She stuck to her guns, though. Stayed single, had a great career as an interior decorator."

"And she raised you."

"At that point, it was only the two of us left in the family and she couldn't bear for me to go into foster care."

"And your parents?" He said it gently, as if he didn't want to offend or cause distress.

She glanced at him. "You're careful with people, aren't you?"

"Now I am. Wasn't always."

That touched her. "I'd just turned two when she took me in. I barely remember my folks, which is probably a good thing."

"Abusive?"

"Not intentionally, at least that's what Aunt Sally told me. If she chose to soften the story, I don't mind."

"Understood."

"My mom had me late in life. Like Aunt Sally, she'd been told pregnancy was unlikely so I was a big surprise. Aunt Sally called my parents fragile. I'd use the word flaky. Dad set off on a quest and could still be in Tibet for all I know. Mom died when she volunteered to test an experimental drug being developed by a friend."

"Hm."

"Yeah. I think they were both into recreational drugs and it took them down. Aunt Sally put a positive spin on it for my sake."

"Bless Aunt Sally."

"That's for sure." She took a steadying breath. "Which brings us to the moment upstairs when I almost kissed you."

He lowered the ice pack. "It does?"

"I mean, I suppose a kiss is no big deal, but—"

"I disagree." Heat flickered in his eyes. "We're not kids playing games. I don't kiss a woman for the heck of it. Not these days."

Her breathing quickened. "Then we're on the same page."

His mouth curved in a soft smile. "Not yet. But we're reading the same book. That's a good start."

"We've established that we're not indiscriminate kissers."

"Right."

"I have a reason for not kissing you a while ago." She paused. "There's something you need to know."

His stance widened and his jaw tensed as he physically braced himself. "Okay."

"When I had my first physical, I got the same news as Aunt Sally and my mom. I'd seen first-hand how much Aunt Sally enjoyed her life as a single woman. I decided to follow in her footsteps." She prepared herself for an argument.

His shoulders relaxed. "I can see why."

"You don't have a problem with that?"

"Why would I? It's your life."

"I've had some guys take it as a personal rejection."

"Sorry to disappoint you."

"Just to be clear, I'm never getting married."

His lips twitched as if he might be trying not to laugh.

"Is that funny?"

"No, ma'am." His blue eyes sparkled with amusement.

"It *is*. Tell me why."

"It's just that I've spent so much time working on my proposal, and now—"

"You have not. You're teasing me."

"Yes, ma'am. Just a little."

"I suppose that announcement could seem... slightly premature."

"A tad bit." His gaze warmed. "It's always possible after we kiss for the first time I'll fall to one knee and pop the question, but it's never happened before."

"Then again, it could be the kiss to end all kisses." She moved closer.

"It certainly could." The warmth in his eyes became heat.

She took one more step. "Let's find out." She landed an open-mouthed lip-lock and quickly added some sexy tongue to the mix. Time to get this party started.

13

Holy moly. Nick had readied himself for a sexy kiss. The light of challenge had gleamed in Eva's green eyes before she'd made her move.

He'd underestimated. She was bringing serious heat, scorching him from the soles of his feet to the roots of his hair, sucking the breath from his lungs and sending his blood rushing to a destination south of his belt buckle.

Groaning, he wrapped her in his arms, craving the sweet press of her body, needing—

"Yikes!" She wiggled out of his grasp and stood back, chest heaving as she gestured in the general direction of his crotch. "That thing's *cold.*"

He stared at her in confusion. "Cold? Lady, that *thing* is hotter than a—"

"Not that." She pointed again. "*That.*"

He glanced at the ice pack clutched in his right hand. The kitchen towel had slipped. When he'd pulled her into a bear hug, the ice pack had been part of his otherwise warm embrace.

He looked up. "Sorry."

She took a shaky breath and met his gaze. "Maybe… maybe it's a good thing."

"Think so?" He didn't. He held up the ice pack. "This isn't surgically attached. I can put it down if you want to try that maneuver again."

She stayed where she was and stuffed her hands in her pockets. "I, um, didn't expect to get so... involved."

"Feel like proposing?"

That cracked her up. "Oh, Nick. Your reaction is *so* not what I expected. I've had guys take it as an affront that I don't plan to walk down the aisle. But you...."

"I was relieved."

"You don't want to get married, either?"

"Oh, I do, especially after seeing the devotion between Henri and Charley. But when you said *there's something you should know* I immediately imagined worst-case scenarios. Your big reveal was mild compared to what I'd come up with."

"Such as?"

"That you only have a month to live."

"What?"

"Or if it wasn't that, then maybe you're on the run from the law because you murdered your cheating ex, or your ex is alive but he's a psycho who's killed two previous boyfriends, or during a full moon you become a were—"

"Wait. You believe in werewolves?"

"Not really. I threw that in for the hell of it."

Grinning, she studied him for several seconds.

"You think I'm a nutcase, don't you?"

"No." She took another deep breath. "But I am trying to get a bead on you. You're a creative thinker."

"Me?"

"That was an imaginative list."

"I guess, but to me, creativity is like you giving someone a great haircut, or Jake cooking a terrific meal, or... CJ adding embellishments to a song." He tacked on that last reference to find out how she'd react.

Her gaze sharpened. "I used to have a crush on CJ."

"Yes, I know." She'd said *used to have*, like she wanted him to know it was in the past. "He's the reason I've never asked you out. Figured I didn't have a chance."

"But then he got engaged."

"Just because CJ's out of the running doesn't mean I have a shot. I was playing it close to the vest."

"Ready to lay your cards on the table?"

"I'd say they're already out there. I kissed you back."

"How do you feel about what I've told you?"

"That it's good to know." Fascinating that she'd felt the need to announce it in advance, though. Was that for his benefit or hers? Time would tell.

Maybe she was right that the ice pack had given them what they needed—a pause, a chance to let this attraction marinate while they worked on the tasks at hand.

He glanced toward the trunk. "Want me to see if I can open that?"

"Yes, please. Don't worry if you can't get it open, though. I have the name of a good locksmith."

"I'll see what happens." He gave her the ice pack. "I won't be needing this anymore. Thanks for the use of it."

"How's your head?"

"Doesn't hurt."

"Lean over so I can take a look."

He did, keeping his hands to himself.

She didn't touch him, either. Her warm breath caressed his cheek, though. "The swelling's down." She stepped back without making contact. "I'll go stick this back in the freezer." She headed out of the room. "Want me to bring you some coffee and a cinnamon roll?"

"Maybe later." His stomach was just beginning to recover. "I don't want to get the lock sticky."

"Good point." She continued into the kitchen.

Pulling out a streamlined pocketknife, he crouched in front of the trunk. Then he glanced up at the smiling woman in the picture. "Maybe Aunt Sally's right about you," he murmured, "but I see a woman running to meet her lover."

"Are you talking to someone?" Eva walked back into the room.

"Just myself." He flipped out the smallest blade. "Habit of mine."

"Funny, I have the same habit." She sat cross-legged near the trunk. "I thought it was because I live alone."

"Could be."

"But you don't live alone."

"Did for a while."

"When?"

"Years ago." He inserted the knife slowly into the bottom section of the lock, the blunt side next to the tumblers and the blade resting against the lock.

"I've never seen anyone try this." She scooted closer. "How old were you when you lived by yourself?"

"I ran away when I was fifteen." He put pressure on the blade, turned it clockwise, then counterclockwise.

"From your folks?"

"No, they were long gone. Foster care can be a good solution for some, but I drew the short straw. Not nice people."

"Sorry."

"I survived." The lock was being stubborn. Not surprising after a lot of years in the attic.

"How?"

He glanced at her. "I stole things and sold them."

"Did you ever get caught?"

"Yes, ma'am." He turned his attention back to the lock, wiggled the knife blade. "I wasn't a very good thief."

"You learned to pick locks, though."

"I was decent at that. But then I'd have to take stuff. I dawdled. Didn't want to steal anything that had sentimental value. It was only a matter of time before I'd take too long and be collared."

"You were arrested?"

"And incarcerated. Juvie was better than my foster family, though. And when I was released, a kind judge found me a job." There it was, the soft click of surrender. He turned the knife once more. "Got it." He pulled the knife blade out.

"Woo-hoo!" She scrambled to her knees. "Open it! Let's see what's inside!"

"That pleasure belongs to you." He rose to his feet and stepped back.

She looked up at him. "You really are a special person, Nick Le Grande."

He opened his mouth, a denial on the tip of his tongue. He gazed into her green eyes. Affection shone there, along with respect. *She likes you, idiot. Your story didn't turn her off any more than hers turned you off.* He swallowed the denial. "Thank you, ma'am."

She gestured to the trunk. "I almost hate to open it. I've had fun imagining what's inside. Probably not gold bars or coins. It's not heavy enough."

"Could be bundles of cash."

"From a robbery?" She looked excited about the prospect.

"I wasn't thinking that. I've heard stories about older people who stuff spare cash in unusual places. Like in the dishwasher, or inside the pockets of old coats they don't wear anymore."

"I've heard those stories, too. I don't think Miss Barton was that type. She kept her money in a savings account and left a note giving it to various veteran organizations. Same with the proceeds of the house. I don't think there's cash in here."

"Whatever it is doesn't weigh all that much."

"That's why I think it's clothes."

"That wouldn't be very exciting."

"It would be if it's sexy outfits she wore for her secret lover."

"Miss Barton had a secret lover?"

"Not since I've known her, and she never mentioned anyone by name, but I got the distinct impression she had some sexy times in this house."

"And she dressed up?"

"Why not? Especially if her lover enjoyed seeing her in fishnet stockings and satin corsets. If I'm right, Beth will get a kick out of looking through Miss Barton's stash."

"Assuming you're right, why would she keep it?"

"For the memories. And what else was she going to do besides put them in a locked trunk? Throwing them away would be wasteful and she couldn't very well donate them to the church rummage sale."

"I suppose not."

"Once I open the lid, the mystery will be solved."

"Then don't open it yet. Save it for later."

"No, I'm opening it." She threw back the lid, which was lined with a flower-printed material. Then she stared at the trunk's contents. "Oh. My. God."

_**14**_

A wedding dress. No mistaking that for seductive lingerie.

It was tucked inside a zippered plastic bag that had turned yellow with age and was cracked in several places. One of Eva's friends in beauty school had bought a similar bag and had shared pictures of her stored wedding dress. Otherwise Eva might not have identified what she was looking at.

This dress looked more gray than white, and clearly it had been in the trunk a very long time. She hesitated to take the bag out for fear it would fall apart in her hands.

Nick peered into the trunk. "Doesn't look like sexy lingerie to me."

"It's a wedding dress that's been stored in this trunk for years. Which makes no sense because I know for a fact Winifred Barton was *Miss* Barton. She told me herself that she'd never been married."

"Her mother's?"

"Couldn't be. They wouldn't have had plastic storage bags when her mother got married."

"Is that all that's in there?"

"I doubt it. This is a deep trunk. But if I try to take the bag out, it's liable to disintegrate, and then we'll have a mess."

"What if I move the trunk someplace where it won't matter as much?"

"Good idea. Maybe to my enclosed back porch." She put down the lid and got to her feet. "That's where I planned to put the other stuff from the attic."

He reached for the trunk.

"Hang on a sec. I've only cleaned a path to the washer and dryer. I don't want to set it on a dusty floor."

"Do you have anything to set it on?"

"I do. Be right back." She walked quickly to a closet in the hall and returned with an old plastic shower curtain. "Now that I think about it, I'd rather sort through it on the front porch."

He hoisted the trunk. "After you."

She held the screen door while he maneuvered the trunk through sideways. Then she spread the shower curtain at the far end of the porch where a maple tree provided dappled shade. "I almost threw this curtain away. Glad I didn't."

"Where'd it come from?"

"It used to hang over the claw-foot tub in my bathroom. It's one of the few things I didn't like when I moved in. The tub's gorgeous and deserves a quality curtain. It's on my list."

"There's a claw-foot tub in there?" He positioned the trunk on the far side of the curtain.

"You didn't see it?"

"No, ma'am. Was a bit distracted."

"You should check it out next time you go upstairs. It's a beauty." She stepped onto the shower curtain and lifted the trunk lid.

"Want me to pull the bag out for you?"

"Thanks, but I can do it." Sliding her hands down the sides of the bag, she located the seam at the bottom and tucked her hand under it. "I'm feeling cardboard underneath."

"A box?"

"Maybe several." Scooping up the scratchy bundle of compromised plastic, she lifted the bag, eased it over the edge of the trunk and lowered it to the shower curtain.

"Are you sure that's a wedding dress? It doesn't look white."

"It's white in the folds. I'll show you." She tried to open the bag, but the zipper was stuck. Instead she pried apart the cracked plastic on the top and pulled out a section of the dress's dingy skirt. "See the white in the creases? Heat, dust and chemicals from the plastic have done a job on the fabric."

"That's too bad. Someone wanted to preserve it." He walked around to the side of the trunk. "I'll bet you'll find out who the dress belonged to if you go through whatever's in those boxes."

Leaning over the bagged dress, she peeked into the trunk. Storage boxes of various sizes lined the bottom. A shoe box likely contained shoes to go with the dress. The rest were of various dimensions, some with flowered lids.

She glanced up, tempted to ask him to help her go through the boxes looking for clues about the wedding dress. That would make it more fun. It would also be a bad allocation of resources.

Time to activate her primary reason for bidding on him. "Ready to get the rest of the boxes down?"

"Absolutely. You said they go on the back porch?"

"Yes, please. It's through a door at the end of the hall. You might want to prop it open before you start."

"Alrighty."

"And watch your head coming out of the attic."

He grinned. "Might be worth it to bang up the other side."

"Nick!"

He laughed and started for the door. "Just kidding." He opened the screen and paused. "I can think of much better ways to steal a kiss." Ducking inside the house, he pulled the door closed.

A couple of seconds later, his boots hit the stairs, creating a staccato beat as he charged up to the second floor. Clearly he hadn't taken her suggestion about propping open the door to the back porch.

She shrugged. Reaching into the trunk, she pulled out the shoe box, popped off the lid and took out one of the snowy white satin pumps. Because they'd been insulated by the dress and protected by a layer of cardboard, they'd kept their color. A quick inspection of the soles confirmed they'd never been worn.

Her chest tightened. If the shoes hadn't been worn, then neither had the dress. Could it have been Miss Barton's? If she'd never worn it, her statement that she'd never been married would hold true.

Gripped by foreboding, she put the shoe in the box, closed the lid and set it aside. The trunk contained another eight boxes. Which one held the answer? And did she want to know what it was?

Maybe not, but she couldn't stop now. She pulled out a square one and found a small picture album with snapshots in plastic sleeves. Nobody put together this kind of album anymore.

The plastic had done a number on the pictures, but the two people in them were clearly in love. In some the guy wore an Army uniform. Was that Winifred Barton with him? She squinted at the face. Maybe. Tough to match this twenty-something woman with Miss Barton.

Laying the album beside her, she reached for one that looked like a stationery box. Wedding invitations? It was about two inches thick and light. Empty?

Not completely. One invitation remained. Evidently the rest had been mailed. *Mr. and Mrs. Edward Barton request your presence at the wedding of their daughter, Winifred Jennifer Barton to Gerald Wesley Sutherland, Junior, son of Mr. and Mrs. Gerald Wesley Sutherland, Senior. The ceremony will be held on...*

She noted the date and made a quick calculation. The contents of the trunk had been sitting in the uninsulated attic for more than seventy years. No wonder the plastic was compromised.

Those two in the album had been Winifred and Gerald, engaged to be married. But judging from the evidence, the wedding had been cancelled.

She returned the invitation to the box and reached for another, thinner one. It had a flowered lid and was tied in a bow with a black ribbon. She pulled gently on one end and the bow came undone. Maybe the black ribbon didn't mean what she feared it did.

The official seal on the letter and the date two weeks before the wedding explained it all. *We regret to inform you…*

She put the box back, scrambled to her feet and hurried to the door. Flinging it open, she stepped inside. "Nick? Nick, where are you?"

"On my way down!" he called back. "What do you need?"

"I have something to tell you." She shifted her weight back and forth as she waited at the bottom of the stairs for him to appear.

He rounded the curve, a wooden crate clutched in his gloved hands, his T-shirt damp with sweat. He paused. "Is there a problem?"

"Where did you get gloves?"

"Fetched them from my truck a little while ago." He continued down the stairs. "You seemed really involved, so I just went on by without saying anything. What did you need to tell me?"

"That's Miss Barton's dress. Her fiancé died two weeks before their wedding."

"Oh, no." He set down the crate at the bottom of the stairs and took off his gloves. "That's awful." Shoving the gloves in his back pocket, he came toward her. "What happened?"

"He was in the Army. Died in the line of duty. His name was Gerald."

"Poor woman."

"I had no idea. I thought she'd chosen her single life and relished her free-wheeling sexual adventures."

"That second part could still be true."

"I hope it was. But what a blow, to be anticipating a life with someone you love and then to have that dream snatched away." She drifted closer, craving his comforting warmth. "I guess it's silly for me to be so sad for her. It happened years ago."

"It's not silly. She was your friend."

She nodded. "Uh-huh."

His gaze gentled. "Come here." Reaching out, he gathered her into his arms.

With a sigh, she hugged him back and nestled her cheek against his solid chest. "I just—"

"I know. Doesn't seem fair."

"It makes sense that she gave everything to organizations that help vets, though."

"Sure does."

The deep rumble of his voice soothed her. He held her just right, too, giving firm support without crushing the breath out of her. "You're a good hugger."

"Thank you."

This was nice, but that didn't mean it couldn't get better. She lifted her head. "You know that kiss that was interrupted by the ice pack?"

He smiled. "I have a vague memory of it."

"Think we could try it one more time?"

"It would be my pleasure."

<u>15</u>

Don't get carried away, dude. Nick lowered his head slowly. He might have fooled Eva into thinking he was super-casual about kissing her again. Tough to stay chill, though, when she'd taken the initiative for the second time in a row.

Closing his eyes, he touched down on the velvet surface of her lush mouth. He barely stifled a groan. The sensation hit him with twice the voltage as the first time.

She'd *asked* him to kiss her. Couldn't get more exciting than that. She welcomed him by parting those moist lips and inviting him to explore.

Cradling the back of her head, he held her steady as he accepted her invitation, dipping his tongue into her hot, sexy mouth... dipping in again, shifting the angle, going deeper. *Ah, Eva.*

Her enthusiasm fueled his as she kissed him back. Cupping her firm bottom, he urged her closer.

She fell right in with the program, molding herself to fit right...there. He shifted his hips, tucked his aching package between her warm thighs.

Her soft whimper sent heat rolling through his body and he trembled as desire gripped him hard. After months of craving her, he had her in his arms, ready and willing. If he didn't stop now....

Heart pounding, he lifted his mouth a fraction from hers. "Eva..."

She sucked in a breath. "Don't stop."

"Don't want to."

"Good."

"Have to."

"You sure?"

"Yes, ma'am." *Lock it down.* Heart pounding, he forced himself to put distance between them. Gradually he let go, stepped back and opened his eyes.

Hers were still closed, her dark lashes resting against her pale cheeks, her breathing quick and shallow. She swallowed and ran her tongue over her lips. "Are you absolutely sure?"

"Yes. For now." His voice was as tight as the fit of his jeans.

"Okay." She slowly opened her eyes, revealing green pools shimmering with desire, an image straight out of his fantasy.

He tortured himself by zeroing in on her mesmerizing gaze. "Rain check?"

She cleared her throat. "No rain in the forecast for at least a week."

"A week? Are you messing with me?"

"A little." Mischief flashed in her smile. "Weather reports are notoriously wrong. It could rain anytime."

He took a shaky breath, ran a hand through his damp hair, gathered his forces. "I suppose this isn't totally my call. You did pay for my time."

"So I did. But the contract was for twelve hours of manual labor."

"It was."

"Where we were headed just now doesn't fit that description."

That made him smile. "Let's hope not. And I came prepared to do manual labor. I didn't come prepared for… other things."

"Is that why you called a halt?"

"Not exactly. We could… there are other ways…"

Her breath caught. "I get the picture."

"The thing is, I promised to clear out your attic and dig up stones in your backyard. When I say I'm going to do something, I like to follow through. It's a point of pride."

"Are you suggesting we work first and have fun later?"

"That's not my place. But it's why I stopped kissing you. Bottom line, you're the boss."

"I respect your need to get this job done." She shoved her hands in her pockets and surveyed him. "Even when certain parts of you are ready to party." Her eyes sparkled with laughter.

"Can't very well deny it." He took a deep breath. "Your call, boss."

Lifting her chin, she looked him in the eye. "Back to work we go."

"Okay." He started toward the box he'd left at the foot of the stairs.

"Wait a minute. Why isn't that box dusty?"

He turned to face her. "When I fetched my gloves, I also brought a rag in so I could wipe off each box before I brought it down."

"That's brilliant. I wish I'd vacuumed the floor of the back porch before you started."

"Guess you didn't hear me doing that, either."

"You vacuumed?"

"Just a quick pass. Went looking for a broom and found your vacuum. Hope you don't mind that I used it."

"Mind? You can deploy that vacuum any old time you take a notion. Now I'll be able to go through those boxes without getting filthy in the process."

"That was my thought."

"Nick, I could kiss you. I won't, though, because I respect your work ethic."

He laughed. "Yes, ma'am."

"But I can offer you a cup of coffee and a cinnamon roll in a little while, when you're ready for a break. How about that?"

"Sounds great, although I'm not sure hot coffee is in order."

"Are you talking about the weather or—"

"The weather."

"Ah. Ever drink it iced?"

"Love that in the summer."

"Me, too. I'll make some right now and stick it in the fridge to cool."

"Give me another forty-five minutes and I should have most of it downstairs." That would allow him extra time to digest what he'd previously eaten and be ready for... whatever.

"Should I come and get you?"

"Please."

"Then I'll make that coffee before I go back to sorting through the trunk." She turned and headed for the kitchen.

"See you soon." He tugged his gloves from his back pocket and paused, his gaze following her retreat, his body responding to the seductive sway of her hips as she walked away.

She paused in the doorway and turned, catching him in the act of ogling her ass. "Gotcha."

He couldn't finesse it. "I'm a guy. Guys look. It's in our DNA."

"Gals look, too." She stared at the telltale strain against the zipper of his fly. "For the record, I like what I see."

He flushed. "Thank you, ma'am."

"You're welcome." She sashayed into the kitchen and out of sight.

Whew. Charley used to kid him about his tendency to bite off more than he could chew. Mostly the comment referred to the amount of food he ate or the scope of the heavy lifting jobs he volunteered to handle.

Did starting a romance with sexy, spirited Eva, a woman determined to remain single, fit in the same category? Probably.

Sexual frustration and the pride of accomplishment drove him for the next half-hour. He loved a job that worked his muscles until they ached. Took his mind off a different sort of ache in his privates, although that had subsided to a low hum of discomfort.

He was down to only six boxes when he picked up a lightweight one with yellowed tape across the top and ODDS & ENDS written in black on one flap. As he shifted it to wipe dust off the bottom, the tape gave way and the flap popped up to reveal red satin material. Eva would be tickled if he'd come upon the seductive outfits she'd hoped to find in the black trunk.

Eager to show her, he damn near bonked his head a second time on the doorframe. He clattered down the stairs to the second floor. "Eva! Think I found something!"

The screen door banged. "What?"

"A box came open." He rounded the curve of the stairs.

She gazed up at him. "And?"

"There's something in red satin lying on top."

"Yay! Fingers crossed this confirms that she had a sex life, after all." She held out her arms for the box.

He handed it over. "I figured you'd want to know about it right away."

"You figured right." She carried the box into the living room, set it down on the carpet and knelt beside it. "I've been reading the journal she kept for the months leading up to her wedding."

"Oh, yeah?" He followed her in and hunkered down beside her. "Interesting?"

"Illuminating. She was a sensual woman, which was so obvious to me during the time I knew her. She'd virtuously saved herself for

Gerald and she could hardly wait for her wedding night. I'd hate to think she died a virgin."

"Um, yeah." Nick coughed.

She glanced at him and smiled. "Are you uncomfortable with this subject?"

"Sex? No, ma'am."

"Your cheeks are as pink as they were when Ellie Mae talked about you during the auction."

"It's not the subject matter. It's the individual connected with the subject matter. I have a hard time imagining... in fact, I'd rather *not* imagine Miss Barton... getting it on."

"She wasn't always a little old lady." She turned her attention to the box and folded back the flaps.

"But that's how I knew her. And unlike you, I didn't have conversations with her that revolved around the subject." As Eva delved into the box, he glanced away. Maybe he shouldn't stick around for—

"Oh, my *goodness*." Eva's voice vibrated with excitement. "Look at this."

He looked and immediately regretted the impulse. The red satin nightgown she held up was a combination of satin and mesh inserts. The inserts had been strategically placed to highlight significant portions of a woman's body. The juicy parts.

"Nick, you're bright red."

"Maybe I shouldn't stay here while you sort through the box."

"Maybe not." She sounded amused.

"I'll just go back to what I was doing."

"Excellent plan."

He took the first set of stairs like his tail was on fire. Great aerobic exercise. The second set was tougher to keep the same pace, but he arrived in the attic panting. It wasn't just visualizing Miss Barton in the nightgown that had him by the short hairs. He'd quickly derailed that train of thought.

But he couldn't erase the image of Eva holding up that red satin number. He was half-crazy with wanting her as it was. If she ever wore something like that, he'd go out of his ever-loving mind.

<u>16</u>

As Nick pounded up the stairs to the attic, Eva began unpacking the box and spreading the items around her on the carpet. Winifred's collection included satin corsets in various colors, thigh-high boots, fishnet stockings, crotchless panties and several transparent negligees.

Nick's progress back down the stairs was more hesitant. Either he was carrying something very heavy or he'd figured out he'd have to pass by her to reach the hall. She was going with reason number two. Grinning, she surveyed the colorful array of racy items.

He appeared lugging a wooden crate and walking briskly. On his way through the living room, he cast a furtive glance at the items on the carpet. Then he gasped and froze in a perfect deer-in-the-headlights stance. "Good Lord." His cheeks turned a lovely shade of pink before he bolted.

She was still giggling when he came back through.

"Not looking," he sang out as he hurried toward the stairs and bounded up to the second floor. His voice drifted down to her. "Any chance you could tuck those back in the box for now?"

She swallowed another giggle. "Of course."

"Thanks." He continued up the next set of stairs.

Before beginning that task, she took out the final item—another journal. The one stored in the black trunk had a virginal white cover, likely chosen on purpose to signify Winifred's determined chastity. The vibrant red cover on this one practically glowed. Eva longed to untie the red ribbon holding it closed and dive right in.

No time. Laying it aside, she began repacking the sexy items. By using a battered old cardboard box and labeling it *Odds & Ends,* Winifred had disguised the contents beautifully. Good thing the tape had come undone or this box likely would have been the last one sorted. If someone else had bought the house, the box might have been tossed in the trash unopened.

But no one else would have bought the house, because she was destined to have it. Closing the flaps on the box, she moved it to a corner of the living room.

She'd just retrieved the journal from the floor where she'd left it when Nick came down with another cardboard box. He handled it as if it weighed nothing.

Balancing it against his hip and holding it one-handed, he looked around until his gaze settled on the box in the corner.

She smiled. "Out of sight, out of mind."

"I'm afraid not. The sight of those items spread out on the carpet is burned into my eyeballs."

"You've never seen that kind of thing before?"

"Only in magazines on women I didn't know. This is a whole other level of..." He shook his head. "I don't know what. Do you have a plan for what to do with them?"

"Not really." She couldn't help herself. Watching him blush was too much fun. "Do you have any suggestions?"

"No, ma'am, I do not." His cheeks turned pink. "I get what you were saying before. Can't exactly donate that sort of thing to a local charity."

"But it's all in such great shape. Throwing it away seems wrong."

He sighed. "I'm opposed to wasting things, too, but how do you recycle something like that?"

"I don't know, but I'll figure it out." She held up the journal. "This was at the bottom of the box."

He eyed it warily. "Read any of it?"

"Haven't had a chance, but I will. I'm dying of curiosity." If this journal turned out to be as hot as Winifred's outfits indicated it might be, she'd be wise to read it in small doses, especially with a sexy cowboy on the premises.

"Do you suppose she wrote about—"

"I can't imagine what else if she put it in the same box with her outfits."

His chest heaved. "Yeah." He gestured toward the box. "I'd better take this to the back porch."

"I'm sure it's past time for your iced coffee and cinnamon roll break."

"No point in stopping now. I'm almost done. Give me another ten minutes and I'll have everything out of there except the big mirror and the coat tree. Do you want those brought down, too?"

"I would love that, but the cheval mirror's going to be a bugger."

"Cheval?"

"That's the name of that style, with a tilting mirror in a standing frame. Theoretically you can tighten the screws on the swivel part to stabilize it, but that part's worn. It's gonna tilt."

"Where do you want it?"

"In my bedroom, but—"

"That means it only has to go down one set of stairs. Could you stuff something between the mirror and the frame to stabilize it?"

"It's not recommended. Puts a strain on the frame."

"Duct tape, then? Only has to be on there long enough for the trip down the stairs."

"That could work."

"If the mirror's stabilized, I could back down the stairs holding the base while you support the top. I think it's doable."

"It's a deal. Are the rest of the boxes like that one? If they're light, I could come up and help you finish."

"I'm not sure if they're light or heavy, but it's broiling up there. I'm already sweaty. No reason for you to get sweaty, too."

She could think of a reason, but it had nothing to do with moving boxes. And speaking of sweat, it looked darned good on him, dampening the front of his T-shirt in a vee-shaped pattern from his strong neck to his impressive abs.

If she took a couple of steps, she could shove the material up and lick salty beads of sweat from his abs to his pecs. Then she'd—

His soft moan startled her out of her impromptu daydream. Her gaze rose to meet his. Whoa. The heat in his eyes scorched her from head to toe.

He cleared his throat. "Good thing I'm holding this box."

She sucked in a breath as his intense stare ignited a fire in every one of her erogenous zones. "You could... put it down."

His laughter was choked. "Don't think so. I've punched holes in it."

She glanced at the spot where his hand gripped the side of the box. "Yeah, you did."

"I'll go unhook myself and... calm the hell down." He turned and headed for the hall.

She followed his progress with hungry eyes. "Don't calm down on my account," she called after him.

"That's exactly why I will. I'm finishing the work you paid for. It's a matter of principle." At the end of the hall he turned back to her. "And I'm gonna need your help."

"But you said you didn't want me to—"

"Not with the boxes. With the way you look at me."

"It's not all my fault. You're the one who brought up the subject of sweat."

"Huh?"

"You said you were already sweaty and there was no reason for me to get sweaty, too."

"So?"

Frustration ramped up her volume. "Are you telling me you didn't immediately think about sweaty sex?"

"No. No, I didn't." His voice grew husky. "But I'm thinking about it, now. Is that why you were looking at me like you wanted to strip me naked?"

"Uh-huh."

"I was ready to let you."

"Except you were attached to a box."

"Yes, ma'am. Would've made things awkward." His chest heaved as he took a deep breath. "Eva, I'm caught between a rock and a hard place."

"There you go, talking dirty again."

He smiled. "You're not helping."

She opened her mouth to give him a sexy comeback. Closed it again. "You're right, I'm not. I apologize. I'll go start on the chili for our lunch. Let me know when you're ready for your iced coffee and a cinnamon roll."

"Thanks. Like I said, about ten minutes. Maybe a little longer."

"See you then." She turned away from his hot self, walked into the kitchen and started preparing the chili. What a crazy situation she'd landed herself in. She wasn't sorry. Just... confused.

Only days ago she'd had Nick in her chair as they'd discussed the bachelor auction and his part in it. She'd only wanted boxes moved and stones dug up. Simple. Straightforward. Not so simple and straightforward anymore, was it?

He took a little longer than ten minutes. The chili was simmering on a back burner by the time he walked into the kitchen.

He breathed deep. "Smells great."

"Thank you." She laid a wooden spoon in the spoon rest on the stove. "How soon would you like to have lunch?"

"No rush. Okay if I wash up at the sink?"

"You bet. I'll get our iced coffee." His every move appealed to her. She longed to touch him, but evidently they were a combustible combo and she needed to curb that urge, at least for now.

She put ice in two tall glasses and added coffee from the carafe in the fridge. After transferring them to the table, she placed a cinnamon roll on a plate and got him a fresh napkin.

"Will you split that with me?"

She turned to him in surprise. "Why?"

"Because I enjoy the taste, but I don't want a whole one."

She frowned. "Are you feeling okay?"

"Never better."

"Are you sure? I haven't pushed you to drink water. You could be dehydrated."

"I'm not. When I picked up the gloves and a rag from the truck, I brought in my jug. I know better than to go without water in hot working conditions."

"Good. I'm embarrassed I didn't think of that. I should have offered you water from the get-go."

He shook his head. "Not your job. I'm your workman, not your guest. It's up to me to take care of my needs."

I'd love to take care of your needs. She glanced away, afraid he'd see it in her eyes and they'd be in a pickle again.

"Eva? Did I say something that—"

"Don't mind me." She met his gaze. "I have sex on the brain. I never expected this to happen. My friends warned me that a bachelor auction had a sexy vibe. And then you rode in on that horse and... it was like a switch flipped."

"Yeah?" He looked pleased. "The ride?"

She nodded. "I didn't want to admit it. I thought this morning I'd be over my sudden infatuation, but instead, it's worse."

"Or better, at least from my viewpoint."

"But I'm interfering with your work."

His expression gentled. "I love that you want to. But I—"

"You have standards. That turns me on, too."

"Everything about you turns me on."

"Then what are we going to do?"

"Make a plan." He walked over to the table and pulled out her chair.

"Will it end with us having sex?" She slid into the chair.

He scooted her in. "If it didn't, it wouldn't be much of a plan."

"Then I'm listening."

<u>17</u>

He'd died and gone to heaven. Nick couldn't stop smiling as he walked to the knife block on Eva's kitchen counter and pulled out one of the shorter blades for dividing the cinnamon roll. He could level with Eva about the food situation because she was as crazy for him as he was for her. It would be okay.

Taking his seat, he sliced the cinnamon roll in half and pushed the plate so they could both reach it. "Before we make our plan, I have a confession. I ate a big breakfast at the ranch before I drove over here this morning."

"You were already full?"

"Yes, ma'am. Very much so. Garrett puts on a good spread."

"Why didn't you say something?"

"Rafe thought your decision to cook was a sign that you liked me. When I saw how hard you'd worked, I figured you liked me a whole lot and I'd better show my appreciation by eating a substantial amount."

Her eyebrows lifted. "You stuffed yourself to please me?"

"Don't get me wrong. Everything tasted amazing. Normally I might've been able to handle two big breakfast meals. But my stomach was in knots about how today would go. I knew what I wanted, but—"

"What did you want, exactly?"

"This. You looking at me like I'm the best thing since sliced bread."

"Nothing more?"

"Well, logically, if that part worked out, eventually other things would, too."

She smiled. "But you didn't bring condoms."

"Are you kidding? What kind of SOB would agree to work in a woman's home and pack condoms just in case?"

Her smile widened. "You're the real deal, aren't you?"

"I don't understand what you mean."

"You don't pretend to respect women so you can get what you want. You genuinely respect them."

"Of course. I work for Henri Fox."

That made her laugh. "Should I be giving her the credit?"

"Maybe not *all* of it. I like to think I had potential when I arrived at the Buckskin. But if I didn't respect—not just women—everyone, including myself and the critters, I wouldn't be employed there. It's a zero-tolerance zone."

"I always believed that, and it seemed to bear out with the guys who've come into the salon, but I haven't spent time alone with any of them until today. You're the first."

"Didn't realize I was representing the team."

"And doing a great job." She leaned toward him and propped her chin on her fist. "What's the plan, cowboy?"

His body heated. "I really want to kiss you right now."

"That's the plan?"

"That would torpedo the plan. I just had to say it."

"I really want to kiss you, too. But clearly that's not in our best interests."

"I don't think so. Here's how I see it. You bid on me with the expectation I'd tackle two jobs that are important to you."

"No, I bid on you because you rode in on a beautiful palomino and I couldn't let anyone else have you for twelve hours."

"Oh." The urge to kiss her grew stronger. "But originally, you—"

"Yes, and you've accomplished one big job already, despite my interference."

"Except for the mirror."

"And the coat tree."

He could stare into her eyes all day. They were the color of new leaves. "I brought the coat tree down just now."

"You did?"

"That's why I took longer than ten minutes. I wiped the dust off, but you might want to—"

"Where'd you put it?"

"By the front door. Seemed logical."

"Perfect spot. Then the mirror is the only thing left?"

"That's it. Then I'd like to tackle the stones."

"What about lunch? It's already past noon."

"If I skipped lunch, I'd finish up earlier."

"Hm." Her tiny smile said she liked that plan. "You're sure you won't get hungry?"

"If I do, I'll munch on cinnamon rolls."

"Tell you what. I'll leave the chili on low so it's available if you need it." She picked up her half of the cinnamon roll. "Now I'm itching to get that mirror down and be done with the attic."

"Works for me." He took his half. "But don't you want to hear the plan?" He bit into the roll.

"I can guess what it is. Once the attic's cleared and the stones are dug up, we can have fun. Am I right?"

His groin tightened. "After I head back to the bunkhouse for a shower and those little raincoats."

"Understood. Too bad I don't have that item on hand. You could clean up here."

"I won't take long." Quickest shower in history. "But there's one other thing. I mentioned creating a fountain with the stones. Or a waterfall. Some sort of water feature that fits the space. If you want me to do that today, I—"

"It can wait. I'm fine with completing the two jobs I had on the agenda."

"Are you sure?" He polished off his part of the roll.

"I'm sure. But do you *need* to create it?"

"Need?"

"Clearly you're determined to finish the attic and dig up the stones or you'll think you short-changed me. If you feel the same about the water feature, then—"

"I don't feel the same about it. If it appeals to you, though, I'd like to tackle it sometime."

"It appeals to me and I want to help build it." She gazed at him. "I assume we'll be seeing more of each other."

"I certainly hope so." He shifted in his chair. All this talk and no action was having a predictable effect.

"Count on it."

"Oh, I will. So now that we've figured out—"

"You do remember what I said, though, right?"

"About what?"

"I'm not looking for... well, let's just say I'm not looking for a life partner."

"Ah. Yes, I remember." A few hours ago he'd been amused that she'd felt the need to announce it so early in the game. Wasn't quite so amusing now.

"I just wanted to check, because you said you want to get married someday."

"Someday."

"Then I hope you find the perfect woman for you."

"Thank you." *What if I already have?*

"I'm guessing you'd like to have kids, too."

This topic wasn't random and he answered the question with care. "If it works out."

"It will. You deserve that." She made the statement as if checking a box. Now she could relax about the subject of marriage and kids. She'd reminded him of her position. They could move on.

He was more than ready to move on. He'd get the mirror out of the attic, check that box and go out back to dig up stones. He drained his glass of iced coffee. "Do you have duct tape? If not, I might have some in my truck."

"I think I saw some in a drawer. Let me look."

"I can head up there and wipe the worst of the dust off while you're looking for the tape."

"Sounds good."

"See you in a few minutes." He rinsed his glass and set it on the counter before leaving the kitchen. The Brotherhood had a system for loading the dishwasher but she likely had a different one.

As he climbed the stairs, he congratulated himself on not reaching for her, not kissing her during that extended conversation. Hadn't been easy.

It helped that he was a filthy mess. His shirt had been relatively clean when she'd needed comforting after finding out about Miss Barton's cancelled wedding. But now—only a case of extreme lust would override his better judgment about pulling her into his arms.

On the other hand, extreme lust wasn't totally off the table. When she looked at him the way she had when she'd asked about the plan, he'd hooked his boots around the legs of his chair to keep from rising to his feet.

She tested his self-control as no woman ever had. That was a clue that she could be the one. Ah, who was he kidding? He didn't need clues.

He'd been convinced from the first time he'd settled into her chair at the salon. But her crush on CJ had been a problem. Now he faced a far more complicated one.

He'd just finished wiping the dust off the mirror's wooden frame when her light footsteps on the staircase announced her approach.

He went to the open door. "Did you find some?"

"I did." She brandished a roll that should do the trick.

He held out his hand. "I'll tape it. You can stay out there where it's cooler."

"That's silly. I'm not some fragile flower. I've spent time in the attic this week. I know what it's like."

"But—"

"Taping is easier when you have two people, one to hold and one to tape." She stepped over the sill.

"You have a point." Clearly she was determined to help. If he hadn't moved back she would have bumped into him. "Would you rather hold or tape?"

"Tape."

"Go for it." Gripping the mirror's curved frame near the top, he stepped back, extending his arms so she could duck under them as she worked.

Their close proximity ramped up his heartbeat and his breathing, but the ripping of the tape made enough noise to cover it. Maybe.

Why should the attic be more intimate than the kitchen? Likely because the heat intensified her scent, a combination of soap, body lotion and aroused woman.

He was fragrant, too, but not in a pleasant way. His smelly self should kill any sexual urges she had. A guy with class wouldn't reach for a woman when he reeked.

"I figure taping around the middle should be good enough." She'd started on the far side, which put the mirror between them.

"That should do it." He was hoarse. Dusty up here. Yeah, that was it. His vocal cords weren't reacting to an attack of extreme lust. Of course not.

She rounded the mirror, leaning over in concentration. *Rip, rip, rip.* "You're right about the temperature. It's like a furnace up here."

And getting hotter by the second. His jeans pinched something fierce. "Listen, I can—" He paused to clear his throat. "I can finish up."

She ducked under his left arm and her hip brushed against his fly. "That would make it harder."

His laugh sounded like tires on gravel. "Not possible."

She stopped ripping the tape from the roll. Silence.

Well, not quite. He was breathing like a freight train. *So was she.* Nothing aerobic about taping. "Eva? Are you—"

"Going insane?" Straightening, she left the tape dangling and turned, caged between his outstretched arms. Her eyes flashed green fire. "Yes. Yes, I am."

He held onto the mirror for dear life while his heart raced and his cock throbbed.

"And I'm going to do something about it." Clutching his sweat-soaked T-shirt in both hands, she yanked it from the waistband of his jeans.

18

Breathing in the arousing scent of Nick's raw masculinity, Eva shoved his T-shirt up to his neck, determined to lick the salty sweat from his heaving chest.

She never got there. He took charge, gripping her head and capturing her mouth in a searing kiss. He dived deep, demanding everything she had to give. She willingly gave it, wrapping one leg around his thigh and welcoming the urgent thrust of his hips.

He let up only long enough to pull off her shirt and his. Then he was back, his tongue in her mouth and his big calloused hands... everywhere.

In seconds her bra joined the two shirts on the floor. She toed off her boots while he unzipped her jeans. She'd never been stripped so fast or been so eager to return the favor.

He didn't give her the chance. She'd only managed to unfasten his belt when he picked her up and deposited her gently on the clothes he'd strewn on the attic floor.

Straddling her, he held her wrists captive as he delved into her mouth, kissing her with an intensity that made her dizzy with wanting him. She struggled against his restraint.

He lifted his lips a fraction from hers. "Stop."

"Then take off your jeans."

"No."

"I want to touch you."

He gulped for air. "Next time." He nuzzled the hollow of her neck, lapping at the sweat pooling there. His and hers. It fell like raindrops from his brow as he moved lower, catching her nipple in his teeth, rolling it between his tongue and the roof of his mouth.

She moaned and arched upward, wanting more. And he responded, drawing her breast into his hungry mouth and sucking until her core tightened and her hips shifted restlessly against the hard attic floor.

Releasing her wrists, he threaded his fingers through hers as he continued to make love to her breasts. She could slip her hands free, but she no longer wanted to. Holding hands created a tender link between them as he kissed his way down her sweat-slick body, his damp chest hair brushing her sensitized skin.

Inch by inch, he shifted his position downward. Her aching need intensified with every passing second. *Please.* She trembled with anticipation.

At last he slid his fingers free and cupped his hands under her bottom. Her heartbeat thrummed in her ears and she dragged in air.

Wedging his broad shoulders between her thighs, he lifted her hips, his breath hot against her moist center. Slowly, with devastating accuracy, he bestowed the kiss she'd longed for. The press of his lips and the swipe of his tongue brought a moan of pleasure. Desperate for release, she thrust her fingers into his wet hair.

He bore down, his talented tongue doing all the right things as the spring tightened within her core. She pressed her fingertips into his scalp and began to pant.

The first wave rolled through her and she cried out. The second wave was stronger. With the third, she shouted his name and arched her back, glorying in the race to the ultimate triumph... there, there. *Now.*

Her orgasm arrived with such force that she almost blacked out. Spasms rocked her body again and again as he held her tight, stayed with her, prolonged the pleasure.

Gradually the waves receded, leaving her more relaxed than she'd ever been in her life. She cleared her throat. "That...was unexpected."

His chuckle was low and intimate. "Yes, ma'am."

"Clearly I need to tape more mirrors."

"Only if you'll let me help." The denim of his jeans rustled as he shifted position and straddled her again. He braced himself on his forearms, his smile lighting his eyes. "That was big fun."

"But a little one-sided."

"Ask me if I care." His gaze roamed her face and breasts. "It's reward enough to see you like this."

She grinned. "A total wreck?"

"A beautiful, sensual, wreck. Your eyes are glowing. Your skin, too." He trailed a finger over her cheek. "I'll never forget how you look right now."

She caught his hand and kissed his palm. "It's all your fault. I tried to control myself. Then I just snapped."

"How's that possible? I'm filthy and I stink. I can't imagine what—"

"This is a first for me, FYI."

"Having sex in a hot dusty attic? Same here."

"That, too. But this is the first time I've turned into a maniac because of the way a man smelled. I've heard friends say that their guy's body odor turns them on. I thought they were kidding."

His eyes widened. "Are you telling me you *like* the way I smell?"

"I don't just like it." She scratched her fingernails down his furred chest. "It gets me hot. Ravenous."

His eyes darkened. "Noticed that. And once you lost it, I lost it."

She smiled. "Noticed that."

"I couldn't have stopped if someone had turned a fire hose on me. I was out of my mind."

"Not totally. You wouldn't let me—"

"I didn't dare unzip. I might've done something stupid."

"Instead you did something amazing. And generous. Thank you."

"You're welcome. Anytime you want to be tossed down naked on a dusty attic floor and ravished, let me know. I hope you don't end up with splinters."

"I won't. I'm lying on clothes. Mostly. Besides, the ravishing was worth a splinter or two."

"Glad to hear it."

"I suppose it's time for me to move, but I'm boneless right now. I don't feel like putting on my clothes, either. What I want is a shower and a clean outfit."

"Want me to carry you down to your bedroom so you can get started?"

She laughed. "That's hardly necessary."

"I want to. It appeals to me."

"The stairway is narrow. Carrying me down there wouldn't work very well."

"Yes, it would." He pushed himself to his feet. "I'm the one who made you wobbly so I'm the one who should get you downstairs. I'll use the fireman's carry."

"Is that the one where I'd be hanging upside down over your shoulder?"

"Yes, ma'am. Ever tried it?"

"Heavens, no! I haven't been carried anywhere since I was four, let alone while I was ass over teakettle."

"It's fun. I've practiced with the Brotherhood lots of times. We can all carry each other except I'm the only one who can carry Rafe."

"I'm slightly smaller and lighter than Rafe." Maybe it would be fun, at that.

"You'll be like a feather. And you'd like it."

"How do you know?"

"It's a chance to let yourself go, let something happen without trying to control it."

"Like an orgasm?"

"Well, it's not *that* good. But hanging upside down helps your brain. Gets the blood circulating better."

"You sold me. I'm in. What should I do?"

"Nothing. Roll over on your stomach. Go limp."

She stretched out and rolled over. "I'm already limp."

"See? This is the perfect time to try it."

"Should I close my eyes?"

"Up to you."

"I'm closing them. I'll pretend you're hauling me back to your cave to ravish me again."

"Wish I could. But I have stones to dig." He slid his hands under her armpits.

"I wondered if you'd forgotten about those."

"No, ma'am." He took a deep breath and let it out. "Up you go." He lifted her parallel to his body and put his knee between her thighs.

The balance shifted as he crouched, grasping her wrist with one hand and her thigh with the other. When he stood, she was perfectly balanced on his broad shoulders.

He wasn't even breathing hard. "How're you doing?"

"This is freaky. The blood's rushing to my head. How're you doing?"

"My blood's rushing somewhere else. This is nothing like carrying one of the guys. I just made the mistake of looking at you in the mirror."

"Which side?"

"This side." He squeezed her bottom.

"It was your idea."

"I know. Could get me in trouble." He nuzzled her hip. "You taste as good as you look."

"Want to put me down?"

"Not yet. We're moving out."

"Watch your head."

"Thanks."

Eyes closed, breasts tucked against his muscled back, she breathed in his manly scent. "I'm getting hot."

"Which kind?"

"The ravenous kind."

His breath hitched. "Might have to do something about that when we get down the stairs."

"What about digging up stones?"

"Might have to wait." He started down the stairs, going slow.

With each step, she bounced slightly. By the third one, she'd started giggling.

"What?"

"This is ridiculous." She laughed harder. "I can't believe I let you throw me over your shoulder like a sack of potatoes with my bare ass in the air. What must that look like?"

"I know exactly what it looks like." His voice was a low growl of frustration. "I'll thank you not to remind me."

"Jeans a little tight, are they?"

"Yes, ma'am." He gave her a light pinch. "Getting hot, you say?"

She giggled. "Put me down, crazy man!"

"We're almost there. Two more steps. Then we'll—"

"Eva?" Fiona's voice drifted up from the first floor. "You upstairs? I saw you got the trunk open! Is that somebody's wedding dress?"

She froze. "Hey, Fiona! Yep, it's a wedding dress." Her voice sounded like it was coming from a woman hanging upside down over a muscular man's shoulder. "I'll be down in a sec. I was helping Nick in the attic and I... split the seam of my jeans. Be right there."

Nick descended the last two steps, leaned over and set her on her feet.

She reached up and pulled his head down. "Please go entertain her," she murmured.

"Shirtless?" he mouthed back.

"Get your shirt, then go. Please. I need a few minutes."

He nodded and she scurried into her bedroom. Then she quietly closed her bedroom door and clapped a hand over her mouth to smother a laugh.

Holy hell in a handbasket. If she planned to continue carrying on with Nick, she'd have to start locking her front door.

19

Nick shook out his T-shirt, but it still looked like he'd been wearing it for three days straight. Couldn't be helped. He put it on, took a quick glance in the mirror and shrugged. There was no improving that mess.

He grabbed Eva's clothes off the floor, picked up her boots and started down the stairs. Her underwear was still warm. And fragrant. Fiona's sudden appearance had taken care of his woody, but the silky material of her panties and the sweet scent of arousal recreated the problem.

Her bedroom door was closed. He deposited her boots beside it, stuffed her undies in one of the boots and laid her clothes on top. After running a short mental video of submerging his cock in a bowl of ice cubes, he was good to go.

He hadn't succeeded in bringing the mirror downstairs, but guaranteed he'd get those stones dug. With the energy coursing through him, he could rip them up with his bare hands.

Funny how things worked out. Auctioning off his labor had led to sweating like a pig while working in Eva's toasty house, thus creating an aroma that drove her wild.

If he'd taken her on a date, instead, that secret might never have revealed itself. He generally arrived for a date smelling like a rose, or more accurately, a pine tree.

Clearly that was the wrong strategy if he wanted to awaken Eva's lust. He might not have CJ's blond hair or his musical talent with a guitar, but he had awesome sweat.

Did it only work on Eva? What if it affected Fiona, too? That would be awkward. He'd keep his distance, just to be on the safe side.

When he walked into the living room, she stood gazing at the picture of the lady running through the field of wildflowers. Last night she'd fixed her hair so it curled around her shoulders. Today it was in a ponytail.

She turned and smiled. "I don't have to ask what you've been doing."

Damn, he was blushing. "Got all the boxes down at last. Lot of boxes. Took a while. I'm a little overheated." Would that explain his pink cheeks?

"I'm sure." Curiosity flickered in her eyes, but no lust. "So there was a wedding dress stored in the trunk? What's up with that?"

"I'd better let Eva tell you about it. Can I get you something?" He asked automatically, although he had no clue what Eva had on hand. But she'd appointed him head of the hospitality committee so he'd do his best.

"Thanks, but I won't be staying long. I just thought I'd pop over and find out if you and Eva had unearthed anything exciting in all those boxes full of who-knows-what. It would be like hunting for buried treasure."

"Yes, ma'am."

"I saw the coat tree by the front door. Were you able to bring that cheval mirror down?"

"Everything but that. It has issues."

"So she said. Must be what she was helping you with when her pants split."

"Exactly." That was Eva's story and he was sticking to it.

"Actually, part of my reason for coming over was to talk with you if I had a chance." She took a step closer.

"Me?" He took a step back.

"It's about my dinner date with Leo tonight." She was on the move again.

"Oh?" He edged away from her. "Is there a problem?"

"No problem." She took another step toward him. "I'm just really nervous."

"Don't worry. Leo's a great guy. You'll have a wonderful time." He backed up and bumped into one of the wingbacks.

"Nick, am I making *you* nervous?"

"No, ma'am."

"Then why are you backing away from me? I showered and brushed my teeth, so I shouldn't—"

"It's not you. It's me. I've been sweating like crazy and I don't want to offend you with the way I smell." *Or accidentally get you hot.*

"Oh, that." She waved a hand. "Don't worry about it. Doesn't bother me." She stepped forward again. "The thing is, I'm a little intimidated by this date with Leo. He's so good-looking. Of course, all of you are. I didn't mean it like the rest of the Brotherhood is average, but—"

"Compared to Leo, we're average. We know it and he hates being reminded of it."

"Why? Why does he have such a problem with looking amazing? I don't get it. Most guys would—"

"Leo's not most guys." Evidently his manly aroma did nothing for her. What a relief.

She studied her tan loafers for a few seconds. Then she glanced up. "I would never ask you to reveal deep, dark Brotherhood secrets, but I don't know the first thing about Leo and when I tried asking questions last night, he dodged them. I'm flying blind."

"Believe it or not, so are we. I can tell you he comes from Southern California. Judging from the way he frowns when he mentions the area, he didn't care for it. He loves Montana, horses and working at the Buckskin. He also loves Henri Fox and the Babes. If you're searching for topics of interest, those are good ones."

She nodded. "I'll keep that in mind."

"My guess is he'll be interested in learning about you. He'd much rather talk about the person he's with than himself."

"My story's not all that exciting."

He smiled. "It will be after Leo drags out all the details. He's a natural storyteller."

"Unless it's his story."

"True." Nick had met Fiona for the first time at the event last night and hadn't learned much about her. Leo hadn't been talkative this morning, either.

Nick liked what he was hearing now, though. Clearly Fiona viewed Leo as a person of value aside from his handsome face and toned body. Leo should be happy about that.

"I feel a little better knowing he protects his privacy around you guys, too. I don't need his whole life story. It's just a date. I'll—"

"I'm here!" Eva scampered down the stairs barefoot. She wore a different pair of jeans and a green shirt that matched her eyes. "Fiona, gathering intel for tonight?"

"You know me too well." She laughed. "But I didn't come over *just* for that. I was hoping you'd managed to unlock the trunk and sure enough, you did!"

"Not me. Nick."

Fiona glanced at him. "You can pick locks?"

"Some. Luckily this turned out to be one of them." So much had happened since he'd managed that feat and yet it was only early afternoon.

"It was an exciting moment." Eva's cheeks were flushed and her eyes bright. She was always animated—well, except when she'd recently been wiped out by a powerful orgasm—but in this moment, she was supercharged. "The suspense was *killing* me."

"The suspense is still killing me," Fiona said. "I asked Nick about the wedding dress and he said the story was yours to tell."

Eva flashed him a look that said he'd made the right call. He'd take all the points he could get.

She turned back to Fiona. "I'd rather show you than tell you. It'll be much more dramatic. But it's a two-part drama—after the trunk, you need to see what's in the cardboard box Nick found. Beth will go nuts."

He sucked in a breath. "And that's my cue. Time for me to head out back and dig up some stones."

"Okay." Eva's expression was innocent, like she had no idea mentioning the box would agitate him.

She had a devilish streak. That turned him on, too. "You might need to put on some shoes and come out there to show me what you want."

"I think it's self-explanatory. I put in stakes to indicate where I'd like to plant some tulip and daffodil bulbs once the rocks are out of there. Feel free to dig up any others you find in the rest of the yard. If you'd like to scope out a good location for the water feature, that would be awesome."

"Got it. I'll fetch my pick and shovel out of the truck."

"Do you want a bowl of chili before you get started?"

"No, thanks."

She regarded him with a gleam in those beautiful eyes. "Just wondered if you'd worked up an appetite with all you've been doing."

Really? Alrighty, then. Two could play that game. "I'm okay for now." He held her gaze. "Think I'd better go up to the attic and bring down my water jug before I start, though. I got distracted and left it there."

"Want me to run up and get it?"

"No, thanks. I'll do it."

"Just don't forget. Digging stones will be another sweaty job. Skipping lunch is one thing, but I don't want you to get dehydrated."

"I won't. And water's all I need for the time being." He gave her a smile. "If I feel the urge for something else, I'll come in and grab it."

Her tongue made a quick swipe over her lower lip. "You do that."

His breath hitched. She was better at this than he was. He'd better make tracks before she got a rise out of him. "If you two will excuse me, I'll get started."

"Great. Can't wait to see it when it's finished."

"Me, either." He headed for the door.

"Oh, Nick?"

"Yes, ma'am?" He turned.

"I think I left a roll of tape in the attic. Would you please look for it while you're up there?"

A jolt of heat hit him in his privates. "Yes, ma'am. Will do." Yeah, she was *way* better at this game.

20

The minute Nick crossed the porch on his way to his truck, Fiona spun toward Eva and lowered her voice. "Something's going on between you two. Don't bother denying it. Sparks were flying just now."

"Something's going on." She grinned. "I'll tell you in a little bit. How about some virgin cider to take with us out to the porch?"

"I'd love it. I'm parched." Fiona followed her into the kitchen. "I knew this would happen, but not so *fast*. How long has he been here?"

"Long enough." She pulled two bottles of cider out of the fridge and handed one to Fiona.

"Obviously. You're glowing."

"I'm surprised I'm not levitating, too."

"That good, huh?"

"Shh. He's coming back through." She raised her voice and called to him. "Don't forget your water jug in the attic!"

"Thanks. I'll get that next."

"And my tape!"

"Yes, ma'am. I'm on it." His booted feet carried him swiftly down the hall and out the back door.

Fiona glanced at her. "Why are you so fixated on that roll of tape?"

"I'm just teasing him." She gestured with her cider bottle. "Let's go sit out on the porch. Do you want to talk about the trunk first, or—"

"Are you kidding? I want to know what happened in the attic!"

Moments later, after Eva had given a redacted account of the incident, Fiona stared at her in amazement. "The smell of his sweat? That's what put you over the edge?"

She shrugged. "What can I say? His raw, uncivilized body odor called to some primitive part of me and I couldn't keep my hands off him for another second."

"I smelled him a few minutes ago and I didn't react that way."

"It might have something to do with pheromones. It's possible his are wildly attractive to me but not to you."

"I don't get it. You've been cutting his hair since March. Wouldn't that pheromone thing have kicked in, even a little bit during his appointments?"

"I've thought about that. He's always freshly shaved when he comes in and he uses some brand of pine-scented shaving lotion. It could have blocked his pheromones."

"That could be why, then. And the salon is a fragrant place—shampoo, conditioner, hair dye, perms—the list goes on. Pheromones might not stand a chance. Did you notice anything different about him last night, without all the salon smells?"

"Well, yeah. After that dramatic ride, I saw him in a whole new light. Literally. When he walked me to the door, I suddenly realized he's a very handsome guy."

"Maybe the pheromones had a subtle influence on you even then."

"Could be. I'm sure he got a little sweaty riding in. Oh, and then we line-danced twice."

"I read one article that said pheromones are nature's way of pointing you in the right direction."

"This was more like a virtual shove. In the heat of that attic, the urge to grab him was overpowering."

"Has this happened to you before?"

"God, no. I would have remembered."

Fiona smiled.

"What?"

"Nothing." She drained her cider bottle and stood. "Tell me about this wedding dress."

* * *

Two hours later, Eva carried the cardboard box of Winifred's sexy outfits out to Fiona's truck. "I'm hoping Beth comes up with an idea for what to do with them." She deposited the box on Fiona's passenger seat.

"She might. It's her specialty." Fiona gave her a hug. "I'd tell you to have fun with Nick but that's a foregone conclusion."

Eva laughed. "I think so, too. I hope your date with Leo goes well."

"It'll be fine. Like Nick said, Leo's a great guy."

"Can't wait to hear about it tomorrow night."

"I have a feeling my story will be a yawner compared to yours." She grinned and walked around to the driver's side. "See you soon!"

Eva waited until she'd driven away before returning to the house. And Nick. Last time she checked, he was still working in the backyard.

When there was no sign of him inside, she headed for the back porch and opened the door. Her breath caught.

He'd retrieved a battered straw cowboy hat from his truck. It lay on the ground, along with his T-shirt, his pick and his shovel. His bare chest and shoulders gleamed with sweat as he tilted his head back, eyes closed, and gulped water from his jug. His throat moved in long, slow swallows.

Lowering the jug, he glanced in her direction and smiled. "Hey, there. Good timing. I just finished."

She opened her mouth, but nothing came out. Her brain refused to function but the rest of her was oiled up and ready for... anything he wanted. Nick was an Adonis. How had she missed that all these months?

"I took out plenty of rocks. Dug 'em up from other parts of the yard so there'd be enough to make a really nice waterfall."

She tore her gaze from the splendor of his physique and focused on a waist-high pile of football-sized smooth stones in various shades of gray and brown. She cleared her throat. "Great job."

"It was fun." Putting down the jug, he picked up his T-shirt and yanked it over his head and down his chest.

She swallowed a cry of protest.

"Come over and take a look." He grabbed his hat and put it on. "Wait. You're still barefoot."

"I don't mind." She padded down the wooden steps and started toward him. The grass that had survived was dry and prickly but not enough to bother her. "Next spring I'm giving this grass some love."

"It'll come back. I was thinking of building the waterfall a little to the right of where I have the rocks piled."

She nodded. "Good placement. And maybe add some stepping stones leading from the porch to the waterfall area."

"I like that idea. Something smooth and cool that feels good to walk on." He glanced down at her bare feet. "Your toenails match your hair. I didn't notice that before."

"Your mind was on other things."

"Still is."

Shading her eyes with her hand, she glanced up at him. "Fiona's gone."

He sucked in a breath. "I figured. I'll leave in a few minutes, too."

"You don't want a bowl of chili?"

"I want a whole lot more than a bowl of chili."

The husky note in his voice sent a shiver down her spine. "Then why leave?"

"Because, no matter how much you love the way I smell, I can't even stand myself anymore. I desperately need a shower and maybe a shave. A change of clothes is on the list, too."

"Okay, if you must. I'll get cleaned up, too. But you're coming back, right?"

"If you still want me to."

"Absolutely." She smiled. "I could never eat all that chili by myself."

"Then I'll take off. But first, let me know what you think of the flowerbed. Make sure it's what you want."

She crossed to the curved strip of turned earth which now looked like a potential home for tulips and daffodils. "Just what I wanted. Perfect."

"Good." He tugged on the brim of his hat. "I tilled the soil a little. I can bring you compost from the ranch to give it some extra zip."

"Great! I'll pick up bulbs this week. Can't you just picture it? Flowers, green grass and a waterfall."

"A slice of paradise."

"Exactly. A couple of comfy wicker chairs, or maybe one of those old-fashioned gliders with a canvas top, something cool to drink...."

"Someone hot to kiss...."

She turned her head. He was looking at her the way a chocaholic looks at a piece of fudge. "Are you *sure* you want to leave right now?"

He took a ragged breath. "Yes, ma'am. At least my head's sure. My package is telling me something different, which is why I'm not going to risk a goodbye kiss. I'm outta here." He grabbed his pick and shovel from the ground. "I'll be back before you know it, shaved, clean and sweet-smelling."

"Hey, would you do me a big favor?"

"Anything."

"Don't put on your shaving lotion."

"You don't like it?"

"I like it a lot. It's a very nice scent. But it covers up your natural scent, and I like that way better than pine."

"Huh. Okay, then. No shaving lotion. Any other instructions?"

"Don't take too long."

"Believe me, I won't." He started toward the porch steps and turned back to her. "By the way, I haven't given you the full twelve hours of labor. Technically I still owe you about six."

"That's okay."

"Not in my book."

"Well, there's the waterfall project."

He nodded. "That might do it."

"And the mirror's still up in the attic."

"No, it's not."

She stared at him. "Where is it?"

"In your bedroom. I finished taping it and carried it down while you were out on the porch with Fiona."

"I thought you needed someone to help you move it safely."

"I thought I did, too, but then I realized that if I could haul you down those stairs without incident when my jeans were pinching me something fierce, I could certainly handle that mirror. It didn't wiggle and it certainly didn't smell as enticing as you."

"I doubt I smelled enticing after what went on in the attic."

"Then you don't know guys any better than I know women. When I brought your clothes to your door, I would have happily stuffed your panties in my pocket. That sweet aroma was working for me. I was supposed to entertain Fiona, or I might have."

"Then maybe I should just take a quick bath and let it go at that."

"Maybe you should." He hesitated. "Ah, to hell with it." His shovel and pick hit the ground with a clatter and he closed the distance between them. "I'm just kissing you. Nothing more." Cupping her face in his work-roughened hands, he took command of her mouth.

As he plunged his tongue deep, a red haze of lust blotted out everything but a burning need to touch his incredible body. She fisted her hands in his shirt and two fingers went right through. She tugged hard.

The harsh rasp of cotton tearing brought her to her senses. Dear God, what was she doing? Gulping, she wriggled away from him. "I... I didn't mean to—"

"Rip my clothes off?" Breathing hard, he looked down at the gaping hole and flashed her a grin. "Not that I mind."

"I'm so sorry. I don't know what came over me. I'll buy you a new shirt."

"Don't even think about it. I rubbed a hole in the material while I was carrying rocks. The shirt was done for, anyway."

"You're just saying that to make me feel better."

"Did it?"

"No! I deliberately destroyed your shirt. I *wanted* to rip it. There's no excuse for that."

"Sure there is." He held her gaze. "It shows how much you want me. I'd sacrifice a hundred shirts to find that out. See you soon, Eva." Picking up his tools, he left, his stride more purposeful this time.

She stared after him, her lips tingling from his kiss, her body throbbing with anticipation. This affair, if she was ready to call it that, was only hours old. Yet she craved Nick more than any guy she'd dated, craved him enough to destroy his clothes.

That wasn't like her. Or it hadn't been until now. Where was this headed? No telling, but she couldn't wait to find out what happened next.

21

"Heard your truck pull up," Rafe called from the kitchen when Nick came through the front door of the bunkhouse. "Did Eva kick you out already?"

"Nope. Going back over in a bit." He sat on his bunk and pulled off his boots.

"Are you, now?" Rafe appeared in the kitchen doorway, a bottle of hard cider in one hand. He grinned. "You look like hell."

"Thanks. What are you doing back so soon? I thought you and Kate were supposed to be gone all day."

"We had a fight."

"Sorry to hear that." He stood, pulled off his shirt and tossed it on his bunk. He could wash it and throw it in the bunkhouse rag bag or keep it as a souvenir. Might keep it.

"Let me guess. Eva ripped your shirt in a fit of passion."

Nick smiled and looked him in the eye. "As a matter of fact, she did."

Rafe blinked. "No shit." His expression was priceless. Total shock and disbelief.

"She's wild about my sweat."

Rafe busted out laughing. "Sure she is. Gotta hand it to you, Nicholas. You had me going. For a minute, there, I thought you—"

"I'm not making this up. My body odor turns her on."

Rafe laughed harder. "You're killing me, bro. No woman alive is turned on by—"

"That's what I used to think. Evidently it's a selective thing. Fiona came by the house and she had zero reaction to my smelly self."

"But Eva *likes* the way you smell?"

"Loves it."

Rafe shook his head. "If that don't beat all. Go take your shower while I look this up on my phone."

After showering in record time, Nick quickly shaved. He grabbed the bottle of shaving lotion, ready to slap some on as usual until he caught himself and put it back on the shelf.

Moving fast, he tugged on freshly washed jeans, a clean pair of socks and his good boots. T-shirts seemed to work for Eva, so he pulled on a white one and tucked it into the waistband of his jeans. As he was buckling his belt, Rafe came out of the kitchen, his phone in one hand and a just-opened bottle of cider in the other. The fight with Kate must really be bothering him.

"I read a couple of interesting articles. You could be onto something."

"What'd they say?"

"It's not just plain old sweat that works on ladies—some ladies, anyway. If the guy is sexually aroused when he's sweating, that's the magic combination."

"And I absolutely had both kinds of sweat going on in the attic, so it makes perfect sense that she'd—"

"The *attic*? Please tell me you didn't seduce that woman in a dusty old attic."

"It's more like she seduced me."

Rafe's eyes widened. "What about condoms? You're not in the habit of carrying—"

"Kept my pants zipped. Just concentrated on making her happy."

"In the *attic*? I'll bet it was over a hundred degrees up there today. Not smooth, bro."

"I don't think she was looking for smooth. But thanks for reminding me about condoms. I was ready to leave without them." He crouched in front of his bunk and pulled out the storage drawer underneath.

"Make sure they haven't expired."

"They're fine." But he checked the date before shoving four into his pocket.

"Is that enough?"

He glanced up. "Rafe, for God's sake."

"Just looking out for you, bro. And living vicariously."

"Hey, I'm sorry about Kate." He stood. "What'd you fight about?"

Rafe took a sip of his cider and gazed out the window. "She can't get past her bad experience with her ex. She refuses to start anything with me because..." He paused and took another drag on his cider.

"Because?"

"Because she knows I want it all. Marriage, kids, the whole nine yards. She swears she's never getting married again. She advised me to look elsewhere. I... well, I said a few things I shouldn't have."

"Like what?"

Rafe looked at him, his gaze bleak. "Doesn't matter. Bottom line, I ruined our friendship."

"Maybe not." He hated seeing Rafe so down. Clearly the guy could use some company and maybe a game of gin rummy to take his mind off his troubles. Nick was torn.

The Brotherhood had established protocol for times like this—*what would Charley do?* Would he have chosen to keep the date with his lady love or hang out with a brother who needed moral support?

"I can see the wheels going around, bro. Get out of here. Go back to Eva's."

"But—"

"I mean it. I'll throw your ass out the door if I have to."

Nick grinned. "You could try."

"And I'd succeed. I'm more dedicated to throwing you out than you're set on sticking around. Vamoose."

"Is there a problem?" Garrett opened the screen door and walked in.

Rafe glanced at Nick. "Nicholas is under the mistaken impression I need company. I don't."

"You want to be alone?" Garrett shoved back his hat. "I can head over to the barn if you—"

"Not necessary." Rafe faced him. "How was the trip to Glacier?"

"Very nice. How was your ride with Kate?"

Would Rafe tell him? Nick wouldn't bet on it. Garrett had been working at the Buckskin since February, but he was still referred to as the new hire. He wasn't a part of the Brotherhood, at least not yet.

Rafe shrugged. "Not so good."

"Ah. I'm sorry."

"Me, too. You up for a game of cards?"

"Sure." Garrett's expression gave nothing away. "I'll get myself a cold one." He walked into the kitchen.

Nick kept his voice down. "Wasn't sure you'd say—"

"I wasn't, either. But maybe it's time to bring him in."

"Maybe. He pulls his weight."

"He does. And now you don't have to worry I'll sit around feeling sorry for myself. Take off, bro."

"Okay." He reached across his bunk and grabbed his keys and his good hat from the row of pegs on the wall. "I might be late." He picked up his phone.

"You and I are riding fence tomorrow."

"I know. I'll be here."

"I could tell you to get some sleep but I'd be wasting my breath."

Garrett walked in, cider in one hand and an open bag of chips in the other. "Should I pretend I didn't hear that?"

"I'm going back over to Eva's." Nick put on his hat, pocketed his keys and picked up his phone. "We... we're getting along well."

"I'm glad it's working out."

"I'll be here to help you with breakfast, though."

"I can handle that," Rafe said. "I'm capable of chopping things. That'll give you a little more time."

"Thanks." He touched two fingers to the brim of his hat and headed out the door. It was decent of Rafe to make that offer. He was thoughtful that way. Damned shame it wasn't working out with Kate.

Sadness about Rafe and Kate stuck with him until he started his truck and Tim McGraw's *I Like It I Love It* blasted from the speakers. Tough to stay sad when that song came on, especially when he was on his way to Eva's house.

Maybe he should text her and let her know he was leaving the bunkhouse. Yeah, excellent idea, *if he had her number.*

How had he managed to spend all this time with her and not get her digits? She didn't have his, either. He'd fix that situation the minute he got there.

The drive didn't take long, possibly because he was pushing the speed limit the whole way. His body hummed with excitement as he switched off the ignition, hopped out of the truck and rounded the hood.

Oh, wait. His phone. He needed to get her number. He turned to go back for it when she called his name.

She stood on the porch wearing silky-looking shorts and a white stretchy tank top. Her feet were bare. Judging from the outline of her nipples under the tank top, she wasn't wearing a bra.

Desire sucker-punched him in the gut. He'd get the phone later. Heart pounding, he lengthened his stride on his way to the porch and took the steps in two bounds. "Need to make sure I get your phone number while I'm here."

"I'll be happy to give it to you." She grabbed him by the belt and tugged him inside. "Right after we take care of some urgent business."

22

Eva's Plan A involved inviting Nick up to her bedroom. Looked like they wouldn't make it that far. Cupping her bottom in both hands, he lifted her off the floor as he rained kisses on her face and throat and cleavage.

She clung to him, cinched her legs around his hips and pressed the damp seam of her shorts against the bulge of his fly. Head thrown back and hands clutching his broad shoulders, she reveled in the eager press of his mouth, the hungry nip of his teeth.

He carried her deeper into the house, losing his hat along the way, bypassing the stairs. They'd be going with Plan B, the nearest available surface. Sinking to his knees on the living room rug, he sat back on his heels, balanced her on his lap and yanked off his shirt. Hers was next.

More hot kisses followed as he pressed her down to the velvety surface of the rug and divested her of her shorts. When he lifted his head, his hot glance scorched her from head to toe. He quickly unbuckled his belt, unfastened his jeans and shoved them, along with his briefs, down to his knees.

Longing gripped her in a tight fist. *Oh, yeah.*

He didn't bother taking off his jeans and boots. Instead he rolled on the condom he'd pulled out of his pocket, his gaze holding hers, his breathing ragged.

She could barely breathe at all. And how she ached. "Hurry."

"Yes, ma'am." Moving between her parted thighs he balanced on his forearms, probed once and thrust deep.

Intense. She sucked in a breath.

"Eva?" He started to draw back.

She clutched his glutes and held him fast. "Don't you dare."

His eyes darkened until they were almost black. "You're okay?" He eased back in.

She gulped as her muscles tightened around his sizable girth. "Very okay. Super okay. You?"

His voice roughened. "Never better." He settled in deeper. "Want me to move a little?"

"I want you to move a lot." She loosened her grip on his firm backside but didn't let go.

"Alrighty, then." His gaze locked with hers and he began to stroke, taking it deliciously slow, then faster, then lazy and almost relaxed. Almost. There was nothing relaxed about the fire in his eyes.

And nothing relaxed about the fire racing through her veins, the blaze that would soon rage out of control within her flushed and restless body. Steady friction drew her closer and closer to her release.

His low, intimate murmur fanned the flames. "Tell me what you like."

Her reply was a breathless whisper. "All of it."

His nostrils flared as he breathed deep and paused. "Almost lost focus."

"Lose it." She tightened her muscles around his cock.

He gasped. "Keep doing that and I—"

"Come on, Nick. Go crazy with me." She squeezed once more.

With a groan of surrender, he changed the rhythm, his powerful thrusts making firm, rapid contact that threw her into sensory overload… and over the brink.

With a startled cry, she fell into a whirlpool of pleasure. As her world spun, she wrapped her arms around Nick's broad back. Eyes closed, he shuddered in the throes of his climax and gasped out her name… over and over.

* * *

Eva lay sprawled on the rug, easily as undone as she'd been after her first Nick-induced orgasm. Except that time, she'd been stripped down and made love to in the seclusion of her attic.

Presently she and Nick were in full view of anyone who happened to walk up on the porch and look through the screen door. Late afternoon sunlight through the windows would allow a visitor to see… everything.

That hadn't mattered when Nick was kissing her senseless and pulling off her clothes in preparation for driving her insane. But this particular party was over.

His warm and slightly sweaty body rested lightly against hers. He hadn't given her his full weight or she'd be squished. His breathing was steady again, though.

Could he possibly be asleep? She'd heard of people sleeping standing up. Maybe Nick could sleep balanced over the woman he'd just gifted with a climax.

She tapped him on the shoulder. "Are you awake?"

"Yes, ma'am." His voice was muffled against her shoulder, where he'd rested his head.

"We need to move."

"I was just thinking that. Hate to. But I need to take care of the—"

"That's not all. If someone showed up at the door, they'd get an eyeful."

Raising his head and pushing himself up another couple of inches, he glanced toward the screen. "Didn't consider that."

"Neither did I."

"You expecting anyone?"

"No, but I wasn't expecting Fiona, either."

"Good point. Close your eyes."

She grinned. "Just because I can't see someone at the door doesn't mean they can't see—"

"I need you to close your eyes so I can make my exit. There's nothing sexy about a guy disposing of a condom, let alone when he's managed to hogtie himself with his jeans."

"Oh." She pressed her lips together but a tiny snort of laughter escaped, anyway. "Sorry. I shouldn't laugh, but you paint an interesting picture."

"Don't think about it."

"Climbing the stairs to the bathroom in that condition could be dangerous."

"Which is why I'm not doing it. You have a trash can and a laundry sink on the back porch."

"Clever. Did you have that figured out when we started this maneuver? Because if you did, I'm impressed."

He gazed down at her. "I didn't have anything figured out except that you were wearing almost no clothes and I had a condom in my pocket."

"Just one?"

He lifted his eyebrows. "Should I have brought more?"

"Hel-*lo*. This is our first night together, and considering our track record, I hardly think one condom is…" The twinkle in his eyes finally registered. "How many?"

"Three, now."

"That's more like it."

"I would've brought all the ones in my drawer under the bunk, but I didn't want to presume."

"Presume what?"

"That this is the start of something and I'll need them all eventually."

She searched his gaze. A hint of uncertainty lurked there. And vulnerability. "It is the start of something, at least in my mind. But I have no idea what that something is. I've never had this kind of reaction to a guy."

"You mean to my sweat?"

"Not just your sweat, evidently. You arrived tonight fresh from a shower and I still wanted to jump you."

"Nice to know." He leaned down and kissed her gently. "Give me to the count of five and I'll be on my way down the hall. Promise you won't look in that direction."

"I promise."

"Thanks." He gave her another quick kiss. "Close your eyes."

She did. It was the least she could do. After slowly counting to five, she rolled to her side facing away from the hall. "How's it going?"

"Let's just say I'll plan better next time."

"Regrets?"

"Not a one. I'd do it all again. I'll meet you in the kitchen in five minutes."

"For chili?"

"Yes, please. I'm starving."

"I'll be there." Getting to her feet, she put on her tank top and shorts while she avoided glancing toward the hall. His shirt was gone so he must have taken that with him.

His hat lay on the floor in the entryway. She picked it up and hung it on the coat tree he'd brought down from the attic. Looked good there, not just because it was a nice Stetson but because it belonged to Nick and it was the one he'd worn during his ride.

Dashing upstairs, she quickly freshened up and hurried back down. The gurgle of water running out on the back porch told her he hadn't beat her to the kitchen.

She took the chili pot out of the fridge and set it on the stove to heat. Serving Nick food when he was legitimately hungry would be satisfying. His famous appetite had appealed to her even before the bachelor auction had highlighted his other attributes.

Turned out he also had an appetite for good sex. She enjoyed satisfying that hunger, too. This relationship was exactly what she was looking for—mutually beneficial with no strings attached.

Nick had been amused by her *I'm never getting married* announcement before they'd even kissed. But Aunt Sally had cautioned her to play fair with her lovers. Nobody deserved fair treatment more than Nick.

23

Nick had to laugh at himself. Making love to a woman with his jeans around his knees was, as Rafe would say, not smooth. Doing it in that woman's living room where cleanup would be a challenge and an unexpected visitor could get a show was crazy. What had he been thinking?

Nothing, that's what. When she'd dragged him in by his belt, any blood circulating in his brain had traveled south. No woman had ever pounced on him and Eva had done it twice.

Even more miraculous, he hadn't been sweating much the second time, at least not until hot sex had opened his pores. Very hot sex. And he'd better get off that topic or he'd never make it through a cozy meal with her.

Drying his hands on a towel draped over the laundry tub, he fastened his jeans, tucked in his shirt and buckled his belt. Next time, he was gonna slow the process down, enjoy the journey. And before he launched into the finale, he'd be naked.

The spicy aroma of chili drifted from the kitchen as he walked down the hall. Now that he'd spent most of the day here, the house was familiar, cozy, even. As he walked into the living room, he glanced around for his hat. She'd hung it on the coat tree. Looked good hanging there, better than when all the hooks were empty.

He could access the kitchen from the doorway near the entry or the pocket door that opened onto the dining room. He'd never used that one and it was closer.

The stove was on the wall separating the kitchen and dining room and she stood in front of it stirring the chili. She glanced up in surprise when he walked in.

"Didn't mean to startle you." But he sure did want to kiss her. "This door was a more direct route."

"Definitely if you're coming from the back of the house. I heard your footsteps in the hall but the living room rug muffles the sound and I lost track of where you were headed. I don't know why I expected you to come through the other door."

"Because that's the one I've always used. Whoever designed this house was smart to put in two doors. You can carry groceries in the other one and bring cooked food out through this one."

"Want to eat in there?"

"Sure, why not? Load me up and I'll set the table." If he had stuff in his arms, he couldn't put them around Eva. If she caught fire, a distinct possibility, they wouldn't eat the chili anytime soon.

"I'd appreciate that."

He'd lost his place in the conversation. Whatever she'd appreciate, he'd do. His stomach rumbled when he smelled warm chili. His cock twitched when he caught a whiff of warm woman. He was ready for action on both fronts. He'd take his cue from her as to which road to take.

She stopped stirring the chili, crossed to a butcher-block counter and opened one of the drawers underneath. "We'll only need spoons for chili and forks for salad." She handed him ornate silver utensils that had the heft of the real thing.

Okay. He was setting the table. "These are nice."

"Miss Barton's."

"Did we use this silver for breakfast?" He'd been so distracted he could have missed it.

"No. Eggs tarnish silver, so I used stainless."

"Didn't know that about silver." He took the two cloth napkins she gave him and a couple of plates to put the chili bowls on. Carrying everything into the dining room, he paused. Pretty lace tablecloth. Long-ass table.

Just to make her laugh, he set up a place at each end. Henri had taught all her boys the basics of setting a table, but everything at the ranch was stainless. Maybe the egg and tarnish thing explained why. Henri wouldn't want to mess with tarnish.

When he walked back into the kitchen, Eva was pulling salad fixings out of the fridge. Taking that job would give him something to do with his hands, something other than caressing Eva's silky skin. "Want me to make that?"

She looked over at him. "Would you like to?"

"Absolutely. Thanks to CJ, I'm an excellent slicer and dicer." Damn. He could have gone all evening without bringing up CJ.

"He's good in the kitchen?"

"Just with cutting up veggies and stuff like that."

She held his gaze. "Does it bother you that I had a crush on him?"

"No, I—"

"Because I think it does. Just now you winced after mentioning his name."

"Didn't mean to. He's a brother and a good friend. If it came down to it, I'd give my life for CJ."

"And I'm sure he'd do the same for you."

"Yes, ma'am."

"I don't know if this will help, but CJ would have been all wrong for me. He's clearly overjoyed to be marrying Isabel and settling into family life."

"Yes, he is." Far from helping, her comment brought up the problem he'd shoved out of sight. With time and luck, maybe it would gradually melt away.

"Besides, my crush on him was based on superficial things. He has blond hair and plays a guitar. I always went for the blond country stars as a teenager."

"I thought you wanted to give me blond highlights so I'd look like CJ."

"No, I just like the effect in general. But now that I know you better, I would never suggest you change the color of your hair."

"Why?"

"It wouldn't fit your personality. You're authentic to the bone. Strong and true."

He swallowed. "Thank you." *Those* words sure helped.

"You don't need highlights to make you look hot. You just are."

He was flattered as hell. And ready to take this sweet-talking lady to bed. Clenching his hands at his sides, he took a shaky breath. "I told myself I wouldn't touch you again until after we had a chance to eat. I'm struggling with that."

"Me, too. But you said you were starving."

"I was."

"Not now?"

"No, ma'am."

Breaking eye contact, she walked back to the stove and turned off the heat under the chili. Then she held out her hand. "Let's go upstairs."

He let her lead him up there, her grip firm. Anticipation played hell with his breathing as he mounted the steps. So many steps. Couldn't possibly have been this many when he'd traipsed up and down them with boxes from the attic.

Eventually they reached the second floor. Her bedroom was only short distance from the landing and he followed her in, his heart a jackhammer in his chest. The first time he'd made love to her, he could only guess how it would be.

No guesswork now. Paradise waited. All he had to do was get out of his clothes and the magic would begin.

Her bedroom glowed in the golden light from the setting sun, brightening the colors of the patchwork quilt on the queen four-poster that took up most of the space. The oval mirror he'd set in the only available corner reflected sunset tinged clouds. A double-hung casement window was open, letting in a cooling breeze.

When she released his hand, he reached for the back of his shirt to pull it over his head.

"Please let me." She grasped his forearms, halting his motion. "I want to undress you."

"All right." He lowered his arms to his sides, dragged in another breath and prayed he could hold it together while she did that. When she tugged the shirt from his waistband, her fingers brushed his sensitized skin and he shuddered.

"Cold?"

"No, ma'am. Excited."

"So am I." She pulled his shirt as high as she could reach. "Duck your head."

He leaned over. She pulled off his shirt. And started folding the darn thing.

"Just drop it."

"No." She laid it on the top of an antique dresser. "I want it to stay right there until you leave. Might as well be folded."

His breath caught. "Until I leave? But that might be—"

"Tomorrow morning? I hope so."

"You want me shirtless the whole time? Even when we eat?"

"Yes, please." She stroked his chest and gazed up at him. "Is that a problem?"

Nothing was a problem when she looked at him like that. "No, ma'am."

"Good." Standing back, she surveyed him. "Let's get those boots off."

"I can—"

"I know you can, but will you?" She grinned. "As I recall, last time you—"

"That's never happening again."

"Sit on the bed, please."

He sat, a position that was not kind to his package in its current state. But he put up with the pain since she wanted to... oh, God, she was going to do it *that* way.

He clenched his jaw as she straddled his leg with her silk-clad tush facing in his direction. Grasping his boot, she worked it off his foot. Her bottom wiggled so invitingly he had to either grab her or look away. He looked away.

After she repeated the maneuver for the other boot and stripped off his socks, she stuffed his socks in the boots and set them next to the dresser. "I'd like those to stay there for the duration, too, please."

"Eva, I'm not the type to parade around the place buck naked."

"I know that."

"How do you know that?"

"You're modest. This afternoon when I came out to check on you, your grubby shirt was on the ground. You picked it up and put it on. Some men would have left it off, even driven home like that. Not you."

"No, not me." She'd been paying close attention. But she still didn't understand a few key things about him. Or didn't want to. That was okay. She liked him a whole lot. And time was on his side.

24

Nick's ripped body dominated Eva's bedroom. His presence added enough testosterone to transform the mood from restful to lusty. Now came the most thrilling part of this undressing routine.

She stepped back. "Stand up, please."

He rose to his feet, his chest heaving. Shoving his hands in his right pocket, he pulled out the condom packages. "Maybe I should put these somewhere."

"I have a suggestion for one of them."

"And I'll be glad to take it. But the other two—"

"Can go on the dresser." She held out her hand. "The room's not big enough for a nightstand."

"I noticed." He put the two packages in her hand and held up the third. "How about under the pillow?"

"That works."

Turning away from her, he slid the packet under the pillow nearest to him.

She followed the motion, riveted by the play of muscles under skin caressed by the sunset's glow.

He faced her and caught her staring. "Was that the wrong pillow?"

"No. I just love looking at you. And remembering what Ellie Mae said about you during the auction."

"That was embarrassing."

"Maybe, but it was another reason for me to bid on you. I bought this house knowing I'd need some help with it. I had no idea who to ask, who would be willing to tackle the jobs. It had to be someone special, someone who would do it with a glad heart."

He smiled. "Me."

"Yes, you." Warmed by his smile, she stepped closer and reached for his belt buckle. "I can't imagine anybody else working on it, now."

"I'm glad." His voice was husky.

Unfastening the buckle, she pulled it through the loops. "I'd like to leave this on the top of the dresser until tomorrow morning, too."

"But not my jeans."

"No, not your jeans. You can keep those and your briefs. Except for right now." She unbuttoned the waistband.

"Maybe you should let me do this last part. I know how to ease them off so I won't—"

"I'll be careful."

"Okay." Arms at his sides, he took a long, shaky breath and stared straight ahead. "Go for it."

Heart thudding, she slowly drew the zipper down. Not easy when he was fully aroused. So was she. Hot. Aching. Breathless.

Hands trembling, she grasped the waistband of his jeans and gently tugged, working the material past his hips. His knit briefs, light gray, barely contained his manly attributes.

Gulping, she crouched, which put her at eye level with his magnificence. She pushed his jeans over his toned calves. "Lift—" She cleared her throat. "Lift your foot."

His voice was strained. "Which one?"

"Either."

He chose the left and she pulled off that pant leg. Shifting, he lifted his right foot and she freed that leg, too. Even his feet were beautiful.

Shoving his jeans aside, she stood, her breath ragged. Last, but not least...she peeled off his briefs, gradually freeing his rigid cock. A drop of moisture appeared on the tip. Mesmerizing. The hollow ache in her core intensified.

He sucked in air. "Eva..."

She looked up. Jaw clenched and neck muscles bulging, he was clearly fighting to maintain control. She crouched down again and quickly yanked his briefs to his ankles. "Step out."

Glancing down, he kicked the briefs away, grasped her by the shoulders and pulled her upright. "I need you." His kiss tasted of desperation, the kiss of a man at the end of his rope.

His urgency matched hers. As he delved into her mouth. she pushed her shorts over her hips. As they fell to the floor, she broke away from his kiss long enough to step out of them and strip off her tank top.

Scooping her into his arms, he laid her on the bed and followed her down, pinning her to the mattress as he reached under the pillow.

"Got it."

"Let me put it on."

"What? No, Eva, I need—"

"Please. Roll on your back. I'll be quick."

His laughter was breathless as he rolled to his back and handed her the packet. "You're playing with fire."

She scrambled up and straddled his thighs. "I won't waste time. I want this as much as you." She ripped open the packet.

"I don't believe it."

"You will." She lovingly rolled the condom down his impressive length. "There you go." Rising to her knees, she spread her palms on his delectable pecs and held his gaze. "Brace yourself. I'm coming aboard."

Heat flared in his eyes. "Please do."

She made the connection with ease, his sword to her sheath. In one swift motion, she took him up to the hilt.

He gasped and swore under his breath.

Leaning forward, she feathered a kiss over his parted lips. "Problem?"

"Uh-huh." He clamped both hands around her hips. "I thought you'd ease into it. I almost came. Hold still, please."

"Happy to. Gives me a chance to thank you." She nibbled on his mouth. "I loved undressing you."

He swallowed. "I loved it, too."

"You did?"

"New experience." He tightened his grip. "Like you were... unwrapping me."

"I was." Raising her head, she looked into his heavy-lidded eyes. "You're a gift."

His breath caught. "Hope so."

"I know so. Gonna turn me loose so I can move?"

"Can't promise I'll last long."

"Can't promise I will, either."

Relinquishing his hold, he slid his hands up her body and cupped her breasts. "I crave you. Every single inch."

"Backatcha, cowboy." Slowly she lifted her hips and brought them back down. "How's that motion treatin' you?"

"Like a match to tinder."

"Let's light 'er up." No point in messing around. She set a rapid pace, reveling in the intense sensation and the pure joy of making love to this wonderful man.

He grabbed her hips again, but this time to urge her on. His chest glistened with sweat as his breathing roughened. She gasped as the first spasm hit.

He groaned. "Felt that. Now I'm... Eva..."

"Here we go, Nick." She rode him harder. "Here we *go*." She exploded at the same moment he thrust upward with a wild cry.

The rhythmic pulse of his climax blended with the waves rolling through her core. Closing her eyes, she gave herself over to the moment, to the perfect connection.

But as her breathing slowed, and the haze cleared from her endorphin-soaked brain, her stomach growled.

Then Nick's did. He chuckled. "I think it's time to eat that chili."

Leaning down, she gave him a soft kiss. "And apple pie for dessert?"

"You're talking my language."

"Am I finally going to see the legendary Nick appetite emerge?"

"I suppose you are." He stroked her back. "But the truth is, I'm not the same man who walked into this house today."

"In what way?"

"Before this day started, I would have sworn that eating a delicious meal was my favorite thing to do. That's no longer the case."

"Let me guess. Making love has moved to the top position?"

"Yes, ma'am." He cupped her face in both hands. "Not just making love. Making love with you."

"That's nice of you to say."

"And nice of you to do."

She laughed. "Oh, I'm generous that way."

"You are generous, Eva." His tone grew serious. "You hold nothing back. When I'm deep inside you, I can feel you giving me everything you've got."

"I do?"

"You don't think so?"

"I haven't thought about it." But now she would.

"Take my word for it. When we make love, you're all in. Thank you for that."

"You're welcome." She gave him a quick kiss. "Let's go make that chili disappear." All in, huh? She liked him a whole lot and their lovemaking was amazing. But all in? That had a ring of commitment. Not the sound she wanted to hear.

25

Nick finally remembered to get his phone from the truck, although he kept his promise and jogged out there barefoot and shirtless. Good thing it was dark. While the chili was heating, they exchanged numbers and finished getting dinner ready.

He got the reaction he'd wanted from arranging the place settings at opposite ends of the long table. She thought it was hysterical.

"Now that I made you laugh, I'll move one."

"No, leave it." She put down the bowl of crackers she'd brought in. "It's like a scene in a movie."

"All right." He'd rather sit closer to her, but if the setup tickled her fancy, he'd go along. He fetched the bowls of chili, left one on the plate closest to the kitchen and the other on the far end. "Which spot do you want?

"The one closest to the kitchen door, please. I'll grab the salads if you'll bring the cider. I'll get us each a fancy glass, too. And we should light the candles."

"It's not very romantic to be ten feet apart."

She grinned. "Absence makes the heart grow fonder."

"What about the bowl of crackers?"

"Good point. I'll bring out a second bowl so we can divvy them up."

"Or I could just move my stuff down to this end."

"Nah, let's do this. It'll be fun. Besides, if we're ten feet from each other we stand a better chance of actually eating this meal."

He smiled. "I'll agree with that."

A few minutes later, after taking a bite of her delicious chili and praising it to the skies, he gazed down the length of a table that seemed to have grown several feet. "You're really far away."

"So are you, but this is good. While we eat, we can talk about what comes next." She started on her salad.

"Well, I was thinking we could have fun in that claw-foot tub. And then—"

"I mean tomorrow."

"You want to see me tomorrow?" That was encouraging.

"I have the day off. The salon's closed on Mondays. But I'm guessing you—"

"Yeah, I'm working all day. But I'm free tomorrow night."

"I'm not. I'm getting together with Beth and Fiona so we can..." She paused. "I mean, we usually have dinner once a week, and—"

"Hey, you don't have to dance around the subject. I'd be surprised if you and your friends didn't compare notes after you've met up with your bachelors. Guys do the same." He dug into his chili. Making love to her was better, but the chili tasted damn good.

"I won't be giving them intimate details."

He swallowed a bite. "You can tell them anything you want. That's up to you."

"You're not worried about—"

"What kind of guy tries to muzzle his girlfriend?" He glanced up. "Am I allowed to call you that?"

"Yes, you are, and yes, some guys try to muzzle their girlfriends. Some husbands try to do the same to their wives. And succeed in many cases."

"I can guarantee Charley never attempted that with Henri. She would have gone up in smoke." He hesitated. "Is that one of the reasons you're never getting married?"

"I'm sure that factors in. I've listened to plenty of clients whose lives are dictated by their husbands."

"Doesn't have to be that way."

"I guess not." She gazed at him. "Did anybody notice your torn shirt?"

"Rafe. He thought he was teasing me when he said you'd probably ripped it in a fit of passion. I told him that's exactly what happened."

"You said that?"

"Do you mind?"

She looked unsettled. "I... not really. It's the truth. What else did you tell him?"

"That we had a hot episode in the attic and you're turned on by my sweat. I had to assure him we didn't have full-out sex. He knows I'm not in the habit of packing condoms."

She blew out a breath. "Well, then."

"I'll add one more thing. The conversation was respectful of you. We're a bunkhouse full of guys, which might make you think of locker-room talk. It's not like that. Mostly because Charley was not like that. He civilized us."

"I wish I'd known him better. But he never came into the salon. He was strictly a barbershop guy."

"So were all of us until Lucy talked Matt into taking the plunge in February."

"If she hadn't..."

"We wouldn't be sitting at this long table staring at each other."

"Funny how things work out."

"Yeah, funny." Would they have had this conversation if he'd been sitting within touching distance? Maybe not.

"Rafe must have known you were interested in me or he wouldn't have remarked about the shirt."

"He knew. All of them did, except CJ. I never told him. He's the type who would have tried to talk you into going out with me. I didn't want that."

"That doesn't surprise me at all."

"Speaking of who knows what, did you say anything to Fiona?"

"She picked up on our behavior, so I told her pretty much what you told Rafe, that we had a hot time in the attic and your sweat and pheromones drive me crazy."

"My faro-whatzit?"

"Pheromones. Mammals and insects secrete them."

"To what purpose?"

"Choosing a mate, although humans usually aren't aware of—"

"Choosing a mate? Are you kidding?"

"No, but I wouldn't take it literally. I think it just means we're sexually compatible."

"That's a fact." What a long damn table. He ate faster.

"In any case, it looks like tomorrow won't work out. Tuesday I'm back at the salon, but I—"

"Unless you want me to come by after you get back from Fiona's." He held his breath. He might be pushing it with that suggestion, especially after the mating discussion.

"Just for a couple of hours? Or to spend the night?"

"That's your call."

"I can't imagine kicking you out of my bed once you're in it."

He sighed with relief. "Good. Text me when you're leaving Fiona's and I'll meet you here."

"Then it's official. Two nights in a row qualifies as sleeping together."

"Who says?"

"I do. You hear about one-night stands, but nobody talks about two-night stands."

"Because that would sound ridiculous." He should be happy with a second night and let it go at that. He couldn't. "Is tomorrow night a spontaneous, what-the-hell thing or are we setting a pattern?"

"A pattern of you spending the night on most nights?"

"Right."

"Clearly I like having sex with you."

"Same here." His chest tightened. Would it be thumbs up or thumbs down?

"And having you run into town every night to stay a few hours and leave sounds... disrespectful to you."

Better than nothing. "I don't see it that way. If you'd rather—"

"I'd rather have you stay the night. That takes it above the level of a booty call."

He couldn't help smiling. "Eva, where you're concerned, I have no pride. Put me on speed dial and let me know you want me. I'll be there."

"Why?"

"Because it's not just sex with us. You're not scratching an itch. You want *me*. Maybe it's pheromones and maybe it's more than that, but like I said, when we make that connection, you're all in. I'll take that feeling whenever I can get it."

"Hm."

If they weren't separated by ten feet of table, he'd have a better chance of gauging her reaction to that speech. He sure as hell didn't want her to put him up every night because it was the considerate option.

She took a sip from her fancy glass of cider and put it down. "I'll tell you one thing about talking across the length of this table."

"What's that?"

"It makes the discussion feel weighty."

He doubted it was the table's fault, but if she wanted to blame a piece of furniture, he didn't care. The subject *was* weighty. She believed she was destined to follow in her Aunt Sally's footsteps. Inviting a man for nightly sleepovers might not fit with that program.

He'd retreat for now. "Okay, tell you what. Forget I asked. We'll take this one day—or rather one night—at a time."

She smiled with relief. "Works for me."

26

The following night at six-thirty, Eva grabbed a diagonal parking space in front of Fiona's shop. She'd spent her morning sorting through some of the boxes Nick had brought down.

She'd also contacted Ellie Mae and confirmed a three-thirty appointment for tomorrow. By afternoon she'd been dragging, so she'd taken a long nap.

Nick hadn't been able to indulge in that luxury, poor guy. As she'd sent him home this morning after they'd cooked breakfast together, she'd suggested taking a raincheck on tonight's plan. Predictably, he'd scoffed at the idea.

He'd texted her a few minutes ago while she was driving over here to confirm that she'd contact him when she was leaving Fiona's. He was eager. God help her, so was she.

After shutting off the engine, she picked up her phone and texted him that she planned to leave at nine. He sent her a happy face. She sent him a kiss. Then she silenced her phone because she was acting like a besotted teenager.

The closed sign hung in the window of Fiona's shop but she always left the front door unlocked on the nights Beth and Eva came over. Shifting a container of homemade brownies to her left hand, Eva opened it and walked in, causing the bell above it to jangle.

Laughter and lamplight spilled down the stairway leading up to Fiona's apartment. Beth must be here. Eva locked the deadbolt and hurried through the tidy shop.

"I'm here," she called out as she climbed the stairs. "Better stop talking about me."

"We can't," Fiona called back. "You're the most fascinating topic we have. We've rehashed what I found out yesterday and we could use an update."

"Aw, come on." She reached the top of the stairs. "You guys had dates last night. You know all you need to about Nick and me. I want to hear what happened with Leo and Jared." She crossed the neat-as-a-pin living room to a small dining table where they both sat drinking wine and eating cheese and crackers.

Fiona pushed back her chair. "Yay, you remembered the brownies."

"Of course I did. I promised I'd make some."

She stood. "Ah, but when your body is flooded with happy hormones, your mind could be taking a temporary vacay."

"Stop, stop. It's not like that."

"Don't listen to her." Fiona turned to Beth. "I saw what I saw. Those two were on fire."

"I believe you. Look at her face. It has that orgasmic glow."

"Oh, for pity's sake." If it hadn't before, it did, now.

"Have a seat, lucky lady." Fiona reached for the brownies. "I'll fetch you some wine."

"You don't have to wait on me. I can get it when I put these in the fridge."

"No, let me. You should conserve your energy. Is he coming over later? We wanted to bet on it except we both think he is."

She surrendered the brownies and took a seat. "He's coming over later. I told him I'd leave here about nine and text him to let him know."

"Awesome!" Beth left the table, went into the living room and came back with a small Racy Lace shopping bag. "This has your name on it."

Eva blinked. "Oh, Beth, you don't have to—"

"I've thought of you every time I looked at this. Take it and enjoy."

She opened the bag and pulled out a filmy, knee-length nightgown with thin straps and a low-cut bodice. Shades of blue and green blended into each other in a kaleidoscope of color. "It's beautiful."

"She showed it to me earlier." Fiona poured wine into Eva's glass and topped off the other two. "Talk about perfect. It matches your eyes and your hair."

"I love it." Eva got up and gave Beth a hug. "I have nothing like this. I had no reason to have sexy nightwear, but—"

"Now you do."

"Thank you for figuring that out." She gave her another hug and grinned. "I could say I'll think of you when I wear it, but I'd be lying."

"I hope to hell you're not thinking of me! Come on, we need to toast." She raised her goblet. "To the exciting new chapter in Eva's life."

"Hear, hear!" Fiona clinked glasses with them.

Eva took a sip. "You two look pretty darned happy. Does that mean things went well last night?"

Beth grimaced. "It means we got an early start on the wine."

"That bad, huh?"

"I'll let Fiona speak for herself, but Jared behaved like he was my big brother. The drive-in was fun. Neither of us had seen the movie and we laughed like crazy. On the way there and back, we talked mostly about business. He made not one move to indicate he's sexually interested in me."

"How frustrating." Eva put down her glass so she could fold her nightgown and tuck it in the bag. "Did you consider making a move on him?"

"I might have if we'd had one of those pregnant pauses where you're just sure something has to give. That never happened. When he left me at my door he tipped his hat. I was ready to knock it off his head."

Fiona giggled. "You should have. That would have grabbed his attention."

"I think he really likes you," Eva said. "Something's holding him back."

"Well, I give up. This was the perfect opportunity and he blew it. I think Fiona's situation is more hopeful, in a way."

Fiona shook her head and took a gulp of her wine. "No, it's not. I'm tongue-tied around Leo. He's too gorgeous for words. Ha! That's why I can't say anything when I'm with him. Too gorgeous for words."

"I hear he doesn't think of himself that way," Eva said. "Did you have an adult beverage during dinner?"

"No, because I'd rather be tongue-tied than babbling like an idiot. I don't know if you've noticed, but I get a lot more talkative when I'm drinking."

"We've noticed," Beth said. "That's Eva's point. A little alcohol would loosen your tongue."

"And I could start saying stupid things."

"No, you wouldn't." Eva picked up a cracker and added a piece of cheese. "You're one of the smartest people I know."

"That's what I mean about stupid things. One too many bottles of cider and I'm liable to launch into a discussion of the fermentation process. Or make the case for Pluto being reinstated as a planet."

Eva smiled. "Leo might enjoy that."

"I doubt it. I'm talkative, not witty."

"He asked her out again," Beth said, "and she—"

"He did? See, you don't have to be witty."

"Tell Eva what you said, Fiona."

Fiona took another hefty swallow of wine. "I said I'd get back to him."

"You'd *get back to him*? Why on earth did you say that?"

"I don't know! I just can't think straight when I stare into those beautiful eyes. I want to grab him and kiss him all over."

Eva laughed. "I know how that is."

"Which brings us to you, toots." Beth speared her with a look. "Fiona told me about the attic adventure, so you can skip that part. Pick up the narrative after she left you alone with Mister Muscle."

Eva sighed. "I ripped his shirt."

Her friends happily leaped on that tidbit and pestered her for more. She only gave them an overview, and still the discussion lasted through happy hour and into dinner.

Would Nick be having the same conversation with Rafe? And maybe other members of the Brotherhood? And why not? They'd known each other longer than she'd known Beth and Fiona.

If Nick filled in the guys about last night, that would change the dynamic when they came into the salon. But it would change anyway if she and Nick continued to see each other.

Eventually the topic switched to Winifred Barton, the cancelled wedding and the box of seductive outfits. Beth was intrigued by Winifred's story and loved sorting through the garments, but she couldn't come up with a logical use for them, either.

"Let me think about it," she said as they packed everything back in the box. "What are you going to do with the things in the black trunk?"

"I'll see if the wedding dress can be salvaged. I could donate that, along with the shoes and the veil. As for the rest, I'm not sure."

"You don't have to decide yet," Fiona said. "Something might come to you."

"It might. There's one other thing I didn't bring over. I'll share it once I've finished reading it."

"She left a book?"

"She left a diary of her adventures with her secret lover, whoever that might turn out to be."

"Cool!" Fiona took another brownie. "Do you think you'll figure out who it was?"

"It might not matter," Beth said. "She was ninety-seven, so whoever it was is likely in the Apple Grove Cemetery, too."

"Maybe not."

Fiona's eyes widened. "You think he might still be alive?"

"It's possible. I'm getting hints that he was younger than Winifred."

"Even so," Beth said. "He could still be gone."

"I know. I may not be able to figure out who he was, but it's fun trying. And that Winifred—there was a bold lady who knew how to go after what she wanted."

"I can't wait to read it," Fiona said. "If you can't figure out who it might be, I'm willing to go through the Apple Gazette archives for clues. Does she have dates in this notebook?"

"No, but she references town events. The Gazette has archives?"

"Of course. Most newspapers do. They're digitized." Fiona was clearly in research mode. "Do you think this man was prominent in town?"

"My guess is he might have been."

"Married?"

"I'm not getting that. But I do think he was someone who wouldn't want the whole town to know he was having lusty sex with a woman who seduced him with leather corsets and crotchless panties."

Beth held up her phone. "Eva, it's almost nine."

"I saw that. This has been great, but I—"

"Say no more." Fiona stood. "Go meet your lover."

"I do believe I will. Thank you so much for this nightgown, Beth." She gave them each a hug, grabbed her Racy Lace bag and hurried downstairs.

27

Nick was grateful for the distraction of a bunkhouse poker game with Rafe, Garrett and Leo even if they did spend more time talking about women than playing poker.

"I still can't figure it out." Leo glanced at his cards and laid them face down. "Why did she say *I'll get back to you*? What kind of a response is that?"

"I'm confused, too," Nick said. "She seemed excited about the date when I talked to her yesterday." He didn't mention that Fiona was intimidated by Leo's movie-star looks. She might not appreciate him revealing that and it would only make things more awkward.

Garrett folded his hand, created a neat stack and set them aside. "I'd give her a few days and then maybe send her flowers."

"That's an idea." Leo nodded. "I'll try that."

"I was thinking about doing the same with Kate." Rafe seemed like his old self unless you noticed the defeated look in his eyes. "Not as a romantic thing, but to see if we can at least get back to being friends."

"If it's friendship you're after," Leo said, "I'd go for a big box of chocolates. She likes dark."

Rafe scowled. "I *know* she likes dark. I know she likes her coffee with cream, no sugar, her favorite color's blue, her favorite singer's Brad Paisley and she hates the smell of burnt toast."

"Just sayin'." Leo took a drag on his bottle of cider. "She'd rather have chocolates than flowers."

Nick sighed. "I wish you'd let me talk to her."

"And say what? It's hopeless."

"Have you ever tried pointing out that you're the opposite of her ex-husband?"

"In various ways, yes. Didn't make much of an impression." He glanced at the kitchen clock. "Hey, lover boy, it's almost nine. Have you checked your phone recently?"

"Yep. Nothing yet." He tapped the screen. "Still nothing...wait, there she is. She's leaving Fiona's." He quickly typed a reply.

Leo glanced at him. "Any chance you'll get some intel on Fiona?"

"I'll see what I can do."

"Thanks. On second thought, forget it. This is sounding way too middle school."

"I'll be subtle." He stood. "Just divide up my winnings. I don't want to take the time to—"

"I'll put them aside for you," Garrett said.

"Yeah, get on outta here." Rafe smiled. "It's nice to see that at least one of us has smooth sailing."

He took a breath. "Right."

"You don't?"

"It's...I gotta go."

Rafe pushed back his chair. "I'll walk you out." He followed him into the bunk area and waited by the door. "I thought everything was peachy-keen."

"It is. For now." He loaded up on condoms, grabbed his keys and his hat.

Rafe opened the screen door and gestured for him to go first. "What's that mean?"

"Seems I have a similar issue to yours. Yesterday, before we'd even kissed, she announced she was never getting married."

"What the—" Rafe didn't finish the comment as he fell into step beside him. "Has she been talking to Kate?"

"Maybe. But I doubt Kate has much to do with it."

"Does she have a smarmy ex, too?"

"No." Nick blew out a breath. "She was raised by her great-aunt, who apparently loved being single. Aunt Sally's her role model."

"Is Aunt Sally still around?"

"Died four years ago. She was Eva's only family and they adored each other. Aunt Sally couldn't have kids and Eva's been told her chances are slim, too. That clinched it for her."

"Then why in hell did she buy that big ol' house?"

"It's a lot like the one she grew up in, the house Aunt Sally used to own. Near as I can tell, Eva's honoring Aunt Sally's choices by following in her footsteps."

"But she's okay with having you pop in for overnight visits?"

"Taking a lover is okay, just so I don't get any ideas about marrying her. She values her independence. Just like her Aunt Sally did."

"Hey, I'm all for independence. Henri and Charley were independent as they come, and they made it work."

"We know that, but Charley's gone. Kate never met him and Eva didn't know him very well. We can talk all we want about what Henri and Charley had but neither of those women saw it in action."

"Damn it all." Rafe stared into the darkness, his voice soft. "Why did he have to die?"

"I ask myself that all the time."

"Do you think Eva will budge on this? I mean, now that you two are—"

"I wish I could say yes, but she's convinced staying single is the life she's meant for. The one Aunt Sally groomed her for."

"She sounds as bull-headed as Kate. I've been holding out hope on that front for two long years."

"Think it's time to throw in the towel?"

"Wish I could. But I'm hooked on her. More now than before."

"I never asked this, but have you two ever—"

"I kissed her for the first time yesterday. And she kissed me back. I thought that was the breakthrough. But I didn't want to go further unless she'd had a change of heart, so I asked. Got the wrong answer."

"Sorry, bro."

"I'm a damned fool. She'd have an affair with me. She said as much. I should take that and be happy. I can't." He cleared his throat. "You need to get going."

"Yeah, I do." He clapped Rafe on the shoulder. "See you in the morning."

"Good luck, Nicholas."

"Thanks." He climbed in his truck, started it up and gave a friendly beep of the horn before pulling away from the bunkhouse.

Two years. Rafe had waited a long damn time to have the life he wanted and it was still out of reach. *Two years.* Would Eva hold to her plan the way Kate was sticking to hers? Would he still be driving to her house for a sleepover two years from now?

He turned on the radio. Switched it off again. *What would Charley do?*

Charley had loved quotes, had been especially fond of one from Maya Angelou. He'd written it out in his block letter style and put it up in the tack room a few years ago. Gone now. But Nick could see it plain as day.

WHEN SOMEONE SHOWS YOU WHO THEY ARE, BELIEVE THEM THE FIRST TIME.

Eva had laid out her game plan before she'd kissed him. What had she shown him? That she was conscientious and straightforward. Honest about her intentions. Serious about the life path she'd chosen.

In other words, he'd been warned, just like Rafe had been warned. The women they were crazy about didn't want what they wanted. They'd both ignored the warning. Rafe was two years into his state of denial. Nick was only two days into his. If he was smart, he'd get out before he was enmeshed in a hopeless cause. Like Rafe.

Eva had beat him to the house, not surprising since he'd had farther to go and he'd spent time talking to Rafe. The inside lights were dim.

He could text her and say he'd changed his mind, that he'd realized their goals didn't match and that continuing down this path was a mistake. Then he could drive away.

He shut off the motor. She was inside, waiting for him to kiss her soft lips, caress her body, so eager for his loving. Rafe had stood his ground, refused Kate's offer of an affair.

A little late for taking that stand with Eva. Oh, who was he kidding? He couldn't drive away from here. Not tonight.

The minute he opened his door and climbed out of the truck, his body reacted to that decision with a rush of heat. His steps quickened as he rounded the hood and started up the walk.

The view through the screen door, even from the walkway, would give visitors some idea of what was going on inside, especially during the day. They'd been lucky no one had dropped by during that episode on the living room rug.

His groin tightened and he winced as he bounded up to the porch. Was she in there? The jeweled tones of the Tiffany-style lamps cast beautiful patterns but the room was largely in shadow. No movement of any kind.

Walking in didn't seem right. Knocking wasn't much better and ringing the doorbell would be worse. He settled on calling her name. "Eva?"

"I'm here!" The patter of her bare feet on the stairs indicated she was coming down from her bedroom. "Come in!"

Had she been setting the stage? His heart twisted. She loved being with him. No question there.

He opened the screen door and stepped inside. "I was slightly delayed. Rafe and I—"

"I'm glad you were." She emerged from the shadows of the staircase. "It gave me a chance to change." She walked toward him.

He forgot to breathe. The glow from the porch light fell on an angel from another dimension, a blue-haired, green-eyed creature wearing something made of fairy dust. The nightgown, a wash of iridescent blues and greens, flowed seductively around her as she moved toward him.

She paused a few feet away. "Do you like it?"

He gulped and nodded.

"Beth gave it to me tonight. She wanted me to have something special to wear."

"That's—" He cleared the sandpaper from his throat. "Very special."

"Can I get you anything? Something to drink? A snack?"

"No, ma'am." *Just you. That's all I need.*

"Then if you're good, let's go upstairs. I was lighting candles when you arrived. This nightgown inspired me. I decided we deserved a romantic setting."

Taking off his hat, he hung it on the coat tree. Then he closed and locked the front door. "Lead the way. I'm right behind you." If he could look forward to this kind of greeting every night, did anything else matter?

28

The whisper-soft fabric of the nightgown swirled around Eva's damp thighs as she climbed the stairs. The minute she'd arrived home, she'd raced up to her bedroom, stripped off her clothes and put it on. When the nightgown had slid over her breasts, her nipples had puckered in anticipation. Nick would *love* this.

She'd been right. His stunned expression when she'd appeared had heightened her arousal by several degrees. And ramped up Nick's. By now she could read him like a book. The tense set of his jaw and the clench of his fists told her he was struggling to maintain his gentlemanly poise.

He mounted the stairs behind her, his breathing ragged, his steps purposeful. She didn't need to glance over her shoulder to confirm that his hot gaze was pinned to the sway of her hips and the nearly transparent nightgown shifting over the swell of her backside.

When had she ever had this much fun in a sexual relationship? Never. Her reaction to Nick's physicality bordered on shocking. Last night in the claw-foot tub she'd explored him from head to toe, fascinated with every inch of his magnificent body.

She planned to revisit all her favorite spots again tonight, but she'd have to wait until he was sated and relaxed. He was neither of those things as he followed her up the stairs.

She led him into her candlelit bower—fresh sheets on the bed, covers turned back, pillows plumped. Flickering flames in glass votives on the windowsill and the dresser gave the room an ambiance that no lightbulb could achieve.

The votives were a last-minute addition. She'd changed the sheets earlier in the day, but if he'd been any earlier, she wouldn't have had time to light and arrange candles. They set the tone she was looking for.

She turned to him and spread her arms. "Here you go. Your move."

His gaze swept the room and came to rest on her. "I'd like to start by kissing you."

The rasp in his voice sent a delicious shiver up her spine. "Be my guest."

Stepping forward, he framed her face in his calloused hands. "Thank you for this."

"My pleasure."

"I've been waiting all day." He pressed his lips against her forehead. "Longest day ever."

"Mm."

"Thought nine o'clock would never get here." He touched down on one cheek, then the other, and moved on to her chin. At last he zeroed in on her mouth.

He nibbled and teased, taking his time, yet a current of urgency simmered under the surface, heightening the tension. Combing his fingers through her hair, he cradled the back of her head and tilted it back as he kissed his way along her jawline to her ear.

He tugged on the lobe with his teeth. "You don't wear earrings." His breath was warm, tickling her ear. "Why not?"

"Never liked them."

"Good choice. They get in the way." He trailed kisses to her other ear and nuzzled her neck. "You smell wonderful. Are you wearing—"

"No."

"Pheromones." He ran his tongue around the outer shell of her ear. "I can taste 'em."

"Cannot." Her breath came faster.

"Can so." He licked his way down the curve of her neck to her shoulder. "Tastes like chicken."

She laughed, then dragged in a breath as he slipped the thin strap off her shoulder.

"And you're delicious." He nipped playfully at her skin. "This is five-star dining right here." He ran his tongue along her collarbone, paused to explore the hollow of her throat and moved across to the other shoulder.

When he slipped that strap off, the bodice lost traction. As it eased downward, he shifted his attention to the slope of her breast. Coaxing the straps lower, he gradually uncovered her nipples.

"Just what I was looking for." He leaned down and drew one quivering tip deep into his mouth.

She moaned and clutched his head. *This.*

Sucking gently, he pushed the straps a little farther and the nightgown slid from her body, the smooth material lightly caressing her sensitized skin on the way down. Releasing her breast, he scooped her into his arms and laid her on the bed.

The cool sheets beneath her stood no chance of staying that way as his hot gaze stroked her from head to toe, fanning the flames of arousal. She shifted restlessly. "I need you."

"I need you more." He swallowed. "So beautiful." Breaking eye contact, he bent to pick up her nightgown. "I don't want anything happening to this."

Her heart melted. She would have left it on the floor and worried about it later. "You can hang it on the hook on the closet door."

After locating the straps, he slipped them carefully over the hook. Then he leaned against the dresser and pulled off his boots. "I've never seen you in candlelight."

"We had candles during dinner last night."

He smiled. "This is a little different." He stuffed his socks in one of his boots and reached behind his back to grasp the neck of his T-shirt.

"You're wearing those for me, aren't you?"

He tugged it over his head and down his muscular arms. "Yes, ma'am. You said you liked the look and I need every advantage I can get." He started to put his shirt on the top of the dresser, glanced at the candles and hung it over one of the bedposts, instead.

"I'll admit I'm a sucker for you in a tight T-shirt." She admired the dance of candlelight on his broad, lightly furred chest. "But I like this look even better."

He met her gaze and held it as he took a deep breath. "Glad to hear it."

The intimacy of his low, gentle voice filled her with longing. She rolled to her side, eager for his touch, his kiss, his warm body melding with hers.

His breath caught. "Dear God, when you look at me like that..." Shoving his hand into his pocket, he took out the condoms he'd brought. "Take these. If I put 'em on the dresser they could catch fire." He started to hand her all of them, then held one back.

Putting it between his teeth, he quickly divested himself of his jeans and briefs. Then he ripped open the condom, dropped the packaging on the floor and sheathed himself. "I'm done being neat."

She scooted over to make room for him. "Good, because I—"

"I know." He climbed into bed and eased her to her back. His voice was hoarse. "I know." Moving between her thighs, he slid the tip of his cock into her slick channel, and with one sure thrust, buried it deep.

She wrapped him in her arms, treasuring his solid strength, the perfection of this moment, the wonder of Nick.

His intense gaze locked with hers as he began to move. He didn't ask her what she wanted this time. His instinctive understanding of what she needed thrilled her.

She caught his rhythm and rose to meet each stroke, the liquid sound of their joining a sensual music she craved. Deep within her core, the spring wound ever tighter. Her pulse raced and her breathing grew shallow.

With unerring skill, he chose the moment to increase the pace. His eyes darkened and his lips parted as he coaxed her quivering body closer and closer to the brink. Then he bore down and she came apart with a jubilant cry.

But he didn't stop. Shifting his angle, his breathing harsh, he kept going, catching her as the spinning slowed and hurling her back into the center of the whirlwind.

Gasping and crying out, she came again, her fingers digging into the muscles of his back as she bucked in the grip of a second powerful orgasm. He added his cry to hers, driving home one last time and shuddering against her, claiming his release.

Braced above her, he dipped his head and gulped for air. "Incredible."

"Uh-huh." She caressed his sweaty back as the beating of her heart gradually resumed a normal rhythm and she could breathe without gasping.

He was still panting when he eased away from her and left the bed. "Don't go away."

"Don't worry." Impressive that he could summon the energy to take care of the condom. She couldn't move if someone paid her to do it.

Her eyes drifted closed. Each time was better than the last. Surely they couldn't keep improving on this activity forever, but so far their lovemaking kept going steadily up the chart.

Nick returned and slipped back into bed.

She opened her eyes to find him propped on one arm and staring down at her with a look of fierce concentration. "My goodness." She used her finger to smooth the furrow above the bridge of his nose. "Why so serious?"

"Because I have something to say and I don't think you're going to like it."

A chill passed through her. "Then don't say it."

29

Powered by the most amazing climax of his life, Nick gathered his forces for the most important conversation of his life. He took a deep breath. "Eva, I love you."

Her eyes widened. She opened her mouth, closed it again and swallowed without speaking.

"I don't expect you to say it back. I've been into this much longer than you. I was half in love after the first haircut you gave me."

She still looked shell-shocked.

He took another breath and soldiered on. "I fell more in love with every appointment. The past two days have convinced me this is it, the real deal."

"Is that..." She paused to clear her throat. "Is that the thing I won't like?"

"No, ma'am. At least I hope not. It doesn't require anything of you. It just is. And it's such a relief to come out and say it. I love you."

Tears shimmered in her eyes and she blinked them away. "I'm afraid to hear the part I won't like."

"I probably shouldn't have started the conversation that way." He stroked her cheek. "I could be wrong."

"I hope so."

"One thing I know for sure—we've found something special."

"Yes." She swallowed. "We have."

He took courage from her agreement. "I also know you like me quite a bit. I wouldn't be in your bed if you didn't. You might not be ready to call it love, but I believe it could be, given time."

Her expression underwent a subtle change, a slight narrowing of her eyes, a tiny crease between her brows.

"But that's only if you allow yourself to love me. That's the part I don't know. Will you?"

"I'm… I'm not sure what you mean."

She was sharper than that. She knew what he was asking. She didn't want to go there. He would, though. "There's a danger in letting yourself love me. If you say it out loud, I might ask you to marry me."

She gasped. "Would you?"

"Here's the part you probably won't like. Yes, I would, because I—"

"Stop it. Just stop it!" She scrambled to a sitting position. "Why are you doing this?"

"Doing what?" He scooted up and leaned against the headboard.

"Ruining everything! Can't we just have fun together? This is *exactly* why I told you what my position is, and now you're—"

"In love with you. And you're starting to fall in love with me. I can see it in your eyes when you—"

"I am *not* falling in love with you. I *like* you very much. What we've shared has been—"

"Off the charts, Eva. Look me in the eye and tell me this isn't the best—"

"So what?"

"So *what?* What we have is rare, damn it! I never expect to find it again. That's why—"

"That's why you want to marry me? Well, forget that idea because I'm not marrying anyone, but especially not you!"

"Why the hell not?"

"You love baby animals and you want kids! And I—"

"I want *you.* I don't give a damn if you can have kids or not."

"Oh, you say that now, but then come the fertility tests and the medical procedures and oh, what about a surrogate? No, and hell no!"

Didn't she know him at all? "I thought you heard what Ellie Mae said."

"Ellie Mae?"

"At the auction. When she was introducing me." He held her gaze. *"You can count on this guy. He'll be there for you, no matter what."*

She took a shaky breath. "I heard it."

"Do you really think I'd say I don't care if we have kids and then put you through hell because we can't? Is that who you think I am?"

"No. You wouldn't behave that way. I'm sorry." She looked up and her eyes filled with sadness. "But that doesn't change anything. You'd make a wonderful father. You should have kids."

"Ever hear of adoption?"

Her jaw tightened. "Obviously. I was adopted."

"And was that a good experience?"

"It was great."

"So you know it can—"

"I was more like her granddaughter. She spoiled me, likely to make up for my parents' neglect. It wasn't a normal childhood."

"Join the club."

"But despite your rough beginnings, you want to be a parent."

"Yes."

Her chin lifted and her eyes flashed with defiance. "Well, I don't."

"Really?"

"Yes, really!" Her lower lip trembled. "Go fall in love with someone else."

"*Go fall in love with someone else?*" Anger propelled him out of bed. Red-hot anger—with her, with himself. Grabbing his briefs and jeans from the floor, he put them on as fast as he could. Damn near caught his junk on the zipper.

"I mean it! I *told* you—"

"Yes, you certainly did." He shoved the socks in his pockets and his feet in the boots. "And I didn't listen. My bad."

"Mine, too." She sounded miserable. "I never should have—"

"Okay, look." Breathing hard, he faced her. "We both made mistakes. But telling me to go fall in love with someone else..." He swallowed. "I don't go around falling in love every day, Eva. I've never felt about any woman the way I feel about you. I can't just turn that off. I'll never turn it off."

She stared at him. "Are you saying you'll always—"

"Yes, Eva. Yes, I will." Snatching his shirt from the bedpost, he stomped out of the room and took the stairs two at a time. He was out the door and down the walk in a few seconds, but like a fool, he slowed as he reached his truck. Stopped to put on his shirt.

She couldn't come after him stark naked. She'd have to put on a bathrobe. He rounded the truck and climbed in. Sat there, watching the screen door. It didn't open.

A soft glow from her bedroom window meant the candles were still lit. How could she stand it? Why hadn't she blown them out? Was she expecting him to come back, apologize and ask to start over, minus the *I love you* bit?

He couldn't take it back. Wouldn't take it back. But damn, this hurt. She didn't have to say she loved him. Or even admit she was starting to, although she was. But to suggest that all he had to do was locate a fertile woman and fall for *her...* ouch.

Maybe she thought that's how love worked. Had she ever been in love? Sure didn't sound like it. Truthfully, he'd never been in love until now, either. It had taken this ginormous emotional attachment to Eva to show him what the genuine article looked like.

It wasn't an easy thing to deal with, this business of love. Yeah, alert the press on that one.

It wasn't like hundreds of country songs hadn't brought that message straight to his truck's radio. He couldn't say he hadn't been warned in that way, too.

He glanced over at the door again. She wasn't coming out. And he wasn't going up to that candlelit room. Might as well drive back to the bunkhouse. By now the guys should be asleep. Just as well. He didn't want to talk about it.

Hell, he'd rather not live it, either. But like he'd told her, he couldn't just turn it off. He loved her now and he'd likely love her as he was taking his last breath.

He buckled up and turned the key. Nothing happened. What the hell? Oh. He stared out the windshield at the faint evidence of headlights shining on the pavement—the headlights he'd left on when he'd walked away from the truck, desperate to hold Eva.

He switched them off, for all the good it would do. Where was his phone? Not on the dash. *Please don't let it be in her house.* He ran his hand over the passenger seat and connected with it. Even had enough juice to make a call, just barely.

Rafe was going to love being dragged out of bed to come rescue his ass. He sent a text. *SNAFU at Eva's. Truck battery DOA. Assistance please.*

The reply was immediate. *C U soon.*

He rolled down the window to get some air and unbuckled his seatbelt. Leaning against the headrest, he closed his eyes. That routine lasted two seconds.

Bolting from the cab, he stood on the pavement, hands on his hips. Walking around would be better. Except his boots felt weird without socks. Putting on socks when he was wearing jeans was a royal PITA, though.

Leaving the door open provided a measure of privacy. Grabbing the armrest for balance, he pulled off his boots. Then he shucked his jeans and laid them on the seat.

He'd tugged on one sock when Rafe's truck rounded the corner. The guy must have been doing eighty to make it that quick. He pulled on his other sock and reached for his jeans.

Rafe slowed and switched on his high beams. Then he cut the lights and pulled alongside. His window slid down. "Did she run you out with a shotgun, Nicholas?" His voice sounded choked, like he wasn't finished laughing but was trying to control himself.

"I left on my own." He put on his jeans.

"In your tighty whities? Not smooth, bro."

"I—oh, never mind. I didn't think you'd get here so fast." He zipped up.

"I can take a turn around the block."

Nick sent him a look and buckled his belt.

"Let me get situated."

"Thanks." While Nick tugged on his boots, Rafe pulled to the far side of the street and swung wide as he came back around. After aligning his truck's front bumper with Nick's, he shut off the engine and climbed out. "You decent?"

"At what?" He reached under the dash and released the hood latch. "If we're talking about making intelligent decisions, the answer is no." He closed the door partway, went to the front of the truck and propped up the hood. "Appreciate you coming out here, bro."

"Wouldn't have missed it." Rafe attached jumper cables to his truck's battery and handed the cables to Nick. "Didn't realize I'd be getting a show."

"For the record, I had on my pants and boots when I left the house." He hooked the cables to his battery. "I just didn't take time to put on my socks, and since I had to wait for you, I—"

"Say no more. I hate the feel of boots without socks. You hooked on?"

"Yep."

"I'll start 'er up." He returned to the driver's seat of his truck and switched on the engine. Hopping down, he walked back and leaned on his front fender. "How bad is it?"

"Not too bad. The terminals look fine. It just needs—"

"Not the battery."

"Oh." He sucked in a breath. "Bad. She told me to go fall in love with someone else."

Rafe blinked. "Are you telling me you deployed the *L* word?"

"Yep. Got to thinking about your two-year wait and decided to take the bull by the horns."

"Damn, Nicholas."

"Dumb, huh?"

"Yeah, but you've got solid brass ones, bro. What you lack in smoothness you make up for in cojones."

"Thanks, I guess."

"Try to start your truck."

Nick swung into the seat and turned the key. The engine caught. "That should do it!" He climbed down, walked to the front of the truck and leaned against the fender. "We just need to give it a couple of minutes."

"Yep." Rafe scrubbed a hand over his face.

"Were you asleep when I texted?"

"Lucky for you I was lying there thinking about Kate. I wouldn't have heard your text if I'd been out."

"That was only my first move. Next I would've called. I don't like hauling you out of bed, but I purely hate the idea of asking Eva."

"Understood." Rafe hesitated. "So it's over between you two?"

A knife twisted in his gut. "Has to be, now that I've said my piece and she threw it in my face. There's no coming back from that."

Rafe nodded. "Same with me and Kate."

"Now what?"

"I wish I knew, Nick." He sighed. "I wish I knew."

<u>30</u>

When Nick and Rafe drove away, Eva left her spot by the window. With no other noise to interfere except the rumble of Rafe's truck, she'd picked up most of their conversation. When Nick started his truck, she'd heard Rafe's question about whether things were over between them, but not Nick's answer or any of their final words to each other.

But Nick's answer was a foregone conclusion. Their hot affair had flamed out. Fun while it lasted. Hell when it was over.

Coming down from that high would give her the bends. Nick, too. They'd both pay dearly for their thirty-six-hour adventure.

After putting on a bathrobe, she reached under the bed and grabbed the box the candles had come in. She blew out the flames, still flickering merrily, and tucked the votives inside the box. Throwing them away was wasteful. Keeping them would break her heart.

Without the candles, the room was very dark. She couldn't see the nightgown hanging on the closet door, but it had to go, too. She didn't judge the width of the dresser correctly and banged her knee against it when she walked over to the closet.

Fumbling around, she grasped a piece of the material and followed it to the straps so she could lift it off the hook. She wadded it up and got most of it in the generous pocket of her robe.

With the candles and the nightgown in her possession, she headed downstairs. The nightgown would be trickier to ditch than the candles. Beth would never ask about it, but tucking her generous gift into a bag for charity would suck, anyway.

The Tiffany lamps gave her enough light to navigate toward the kitchen, where she'd left a light on over the stove, the way Aunt Sally always had. The contents of the cupboards were arranged the way they'd been in Aunt Sally's house. A bowl of apples sat on the counter because Aunt Sally had always had an apple bowl.

But it wasn't her aunt's influence that dominated the space, now. Nick's presence was everywhere—overfeeding him at the kitchen table, sharing food prep last night, sneaking down here at three a.m. to finish off the cinnamon rolls. He'd said it was a point of honor. They wouldn't go stale on his watch.

She'd taken the cinnamon roll run as a sign that his appetite was back in full force. She'd confirmed it when they'd cooked breakfast together. He'd been ravenous, both for food and for her. Leaving hadn't been easy for him, but he'd done it.

Leaving had been a snap for him tonight. When his truck hadn't pulled away immediately, she'd fantasized he might be debating a plea to renegotiate. Then Rafe had arrived, making the situation clear. He hadn't stayed because he was undecided. He'd stayed because his truck wouldn't start.

She dumped the votives in the kitchen trashcan. Garbage day was tomorrow so they'd be out of here for good. The nightgown in her pocket was a different story.

She'd never owned nightwear this lovely. But she'd never wear it again. Maybe getting it out of sight was the best she could do for now. And she had the perfect place.

A nightlight on the back porch helped her navigate the hallway. She'd asked Nick to move the black trunk to the porch while she figured out what to do with the contents. She'd thrown away the disintegrating plastic storage bag in her outside trash bin.

Opening the curved lid, she lifted a section of the wedding dress and shoved the nightgown underneath it. Eventually she'd deal with the contents of the trunk, but it didn't have to be now. Or tomorrow.

She had plenty of other items on her plate...like Nick's freaking presence in every *freaking* corner of her house, including this one. How had she let that happen?

Turning on the floodlights that illuminated the back yard, she stared at the pile of stones and the freshly tilled earth where she'd plant her bulbs this week. He was out there, too, of course.

And in her claw-foot tub and most certainly in her attic. Where *hadn't* he made his mark? Only the two bedrooms she hadn't cleaned or done anything with were Nick-free zones. She couldn't very well live in those for the rest of her life.

She was well and truly screwed. Good thing she hadn't fallen in love with him. That would have been the icing on this fustercluck cake.

* * *

Eva slept fitfully but managed to get in a few hours, which she desperately needed to handle a full load of clients at the salon. Josette greeted her with a cheery question about how Sunday had turned out with Nick.

She'd fill Josette in eventually, but not now, considering the number of clients they'd each booked. She responded with an equally cheerful *great* which was true as far as it went.

The first two hours of the morning flew by. Because she loved her work and her clients, she could block out the tragic conclusion of her affair with Nick and simply do her job. Then her eleven o'clock arrived—Jake Lassiter.

He eyed her with caution as he settled into her chair. His *how's it going* had an undercurrent of tension. Clearly the Buckskin Brotherhood hotline had sent out the word—one of their own had been wounded. And they were a protective bunch.

She treated him as if nothing was wrong as she washed his hair and wielded her scissors.

She asked about Millie and whether they'd set a date. Not yet.

He thanked her for her contribution to Raptors Rise and she asked about progress on the visitor center. Henri had hired Jake to manage the sanctuary and he loved the idea of working with wild birds. For several minutes they sailed happily along on that conversational river.

But as she was blow-drying his hair, he lowered his voice and dropped his bombshell. "Eva, Nick's destroyed. Totally wiped out."

She switched off the dryer and took a breath. Clearly he'd used the dryer noise to mask his comment. "I'm sorry to hear that."

"He'd kill me for saying it, but I've been in his shoes." He continued to speak in soft tones. The chatter between Josette and her client provided excellent cover. "I didn't want anybody messing in my business, either, but if they hadn't, I wouldn't be with Millie now."

Her chest tightened. "With all due respect, Jake, your situation with Millie is nothing like mine with Nick." She squirted a dab of styling gel on her fingers.

"In most ways, that's true, but I'll go out on a limb and say one thing looks the same to me."

She rubbed the styling gel into his thick hair. "I can't imagine what."

"The life Millie offered scared me to death."

She fought to stay calm, stroking the gel through his hair, creating a sassy style that he'd ruin the minute he put on his hat. "I'm not scared of what Nick is offering. I simply don't want it."

The tight band around her chest had gone from uncomfortable to painful.

He met her gaze in the mirror, his expression sober. "Then maybe I'm mistaken."

"I'm sorry he's hurting." Between the lump in her throat and her shortness of breath, she could barely get the words out. She wiped her hands on a towel. "He's a great guy."

"He thinks the world of you, too."

"He does? Even after—"

"That's the way Nick is. Once you get the Nick stamp of approval, you'll have it forever."

She ducked her head and clutched the towel as tears pushed at the back of her eyes.

"I've upset you." Jake's kind voice threatened to open the floodgates. "But I—"

"Be right back. Something in my eye." She dashed to the restroom and pressed the towel to her face. Bad idea. Gel residue. Something was in her eye for real, now.

Tossing the towel in the hamper, she turned on the faucet and splashed water in her eyes until the burning eased. Deep breaths. Deep breaths.

Someone rapped on the open door. "Eva?"

Josette. She grabbed a hand towel from the basket on the vanity and blotted her face before turning around. "Stupid move. Got styling gel in my eye."

Clearly Josette wasn't buying it. "Jake asked me to check on you. He looked worried. Took off his cape and got out of his chair. If I hadn't come back here right away, I think he would have."

"He's just... Nick and I..." She dragged in a breath. "Nick and I ended the shortest affair in history last night."

"Oh, dear." Josette started forward.

Eva raised both hands to prevent the hug that was coming. "I'm hanging on by a thread."

"Right." She backed up. "I'll reschedule your appointments, including Ellie Mae's. She'll be back in town eventually, and—"

"Please don't reschedule anything. Working is a good distraction. Especially with someone like Ellie Mae."

"Yeah, but are you up for the processing party? That's going to be—"

"What processing party?"

"Oh, jeez. You weren't contacted?"

"No."

"Classic case of me assuming it was covered. Ed invited the Babes to party at the salon during Ellie Mae's appointment. Henri's my four o'clock, anyway, and the rest are all available. Ed's having it catered by the Moose."

"Do we have room?"

"Ed's bringing folding tables and chairs to create a little café area outside. We'll prop the door open. I said the party was fine with me, and since you hadn't said no I thought it was fine with you, too. I'm so sorry. We can still cancel it."

"But it is fine with me. I warned Ellie Mae it would be a couple hours for bleaching and at least another hour for the blue to process. That's probably why they thought of it. It's a great idea for filling the time."

Josette looked uncertain. "If you're sure."

"I am. Sounds fun."

"Then I'm nominating myself as your assistant stylist after I finish with Henri."

She smiled. "We haven't double-teamed a client in a long time. Remember when we used to do that because we had so few clients?"

"And now look at us."

"We're a hit." She dropped the hand towel in the hamper and held out her arms. "I'll take that hug, now."

31

Eating used to be so much fun. Not anymore. But Nick had forced himself to plow through the dinner he'd helped Garrett fix. Rafe could get away with picking at his food. Nick had a reputation to uphold.

Everyone on the ranch knew he'd crashed and burned because the word always got out on the Buckskin. He'd had enough expressions of sympathy and consoling pats on the shoulder to last a million years. If he stopped eating like a horse, he'd attract even more attention.

They'd nearly finished kitchen cleanup when Matt, Jake and CJ came through the front door, clearly on a mission. Could be anything, but it likely concerned his current troubles, or maybe Rafe's, too, since they both had their asses in a sling.

Leo hung up the dishtowel he'd been using. "To what do we owe this honor?"

Matt thumbed back his hat. "Thought we could use a Brotherhood meeting. Haven't had one in weeks."

"I have to check my calendar." Rafe put the butter in the fridge and exchanged a look with Nick. "I think I'm booked."

Nick put the last plate in the dishwasher and loaded the soap dispenser. "Me, too." He wanted a Brotherhood meeting like he wanted an itchy rash all over his body. "I'm pretty sure I'm unavailable."

Matt walked to the kitchen table and pulled out a chair. "Let me rephrase. A *mandatory* Brotherhood meeting."

"I'll go for a walk." Garrett finished wiping down the sink and draped the dishrag over the faucet. "I'm not—"

"It's fine with me if you stay." Matt took a seat. "You know what this is about and I'd value your insights. Everybody else agree?"

What this is about? Nick cringed. Yeah, he was outta here. He glanced over at Rafe and tipped his head toward the front door. Rafe nodded.

Meanwhile chairs scraped as the others took seats and urged Garrett to stay if he was willing. He sat down.

Leo looked in Nick and Rafe's direction. "You gonna join us?"

Nick edged toward the kitchen door. "Unfortunately, I can't. Lucky Ducky was limping a bit today. Rafe and I need to head down to the barn and check out his right front hoof."

"Hey, Nick," Jake said. "I got a haircut this morning."

Damn it. There was the bait. He took it. "How's she doing?"

"I'd tell you except you're leaving."

He gazed at Rafe, who shrugged, leaving it up to him.

"Look," Matt said. "We'll talk about you whether you're here or not. You never know. We might even come up with a helpful strategy or two."

He shook his head. "I appreciate the thought, Matt, but you're wasting your time."

"Could be." He smiled. "But what else have you got?"

"Aw, hell, bro." Rafe started toward the table. "Matt's right, as usual. We got nothin'. Let's give this a shot."

"Okay, but I need liquid fortification." He walked over to the fridge. "Anybody else?"

"I'll take one," Rafe said.

"Me, too," Matt said, "but just one. I figure after we hash this out, we'll hit the Moose."

Rafe stiffened. "Are we gonna invite the ladies?"

"Not tonight. It'll be just us."

"Okay." He exhaled and leaned back in his chair. "Good."

Nick passed everyone a cold one and settled into a seat next to Rafe. "Let the games begin." He looked across the table at Jake. "Whatcha got, bro?"

"First off, she's in no better shape than you."

"Is that supposed to make me happy?"

"No, but if she's upset, she's into you."

"I know she is. And she's fighting it tooth and nail."

"Because she's scared."

"Scared?"

"Terrified. Pulling into her shell, just like I did when I figured out what Millie wanted from me. I knew I'd fail. I don't know what Eva's afraid of, though."

"Change, I guess."

Matt shook his head. "I don't think that's it. I wish I could've brought Lucy—"

"To a Brotherhood meeting?" Rafe looked scandalized.

"Would've been fine, but she couldn't make it. Something with the Babes. Anyway, we talked about Eva. Lucy maintains she's a risk-taker."

"Yeah, I'd have to agree with Lucy," CJ said. "Eva opened the salon with Josette in an unfamiliar place. Starting a small business takes guts, even when you know the area. Just ask Izzy."

"Buying that house was a bold move, too," Rafe said. "It's a big responsibility and she's lived in the apartment over the salon for ten years. I don't think she's scared of change."

Nick gazed at Jake. "Are you sure she's afraid of something?"

"Positive."

"It's marriage." Rafe sighed. "Just like Kate."

"Yeah, and her Aunt Sally convinced her being single is the way to go," Nick said. "She's determined to stick to that plan."

"Determination is a different animal." Jake leaned forward, his gaze intent. "If that's what I'd seen in her eyes today, I would've advised you to give up on her. But I saw fear, bro."

Matt frowned. "Which makes sense if we're talking about Kate after what she's been through. But Eva's never been married."

"Neither had I," Jake said. "But marriage terrified me."

"Except it wasn't marriage itself that scared you." Nick gazed at Jake as the pins slowly shifted and the lock gave way. "You thought you'd turn into your father."

He nodded. "And I'd ruin Millie's life."

Nick dragged in a breath and glanced around the table. "I know what Eva's afraid of."

32

This was more like it. Although Eva couldn't drink the champagne that was flowing like water, she had a contact high from the rowdy group of women crammed into the salon to watch Ellie Mae's hair transformed from brunette to blue. The front door was propped open so anyone who needed more room could head out to one of the tables on the sidewalk.

Lucy and Henri had each given her a hug when they'd arrived but thankfully hadn't asked any questions about the situation with Nick. Eva had taken Lucy aside to ask if the rest of the Babes knew about the breakup. They didn't.

What a relief. She could relax and enjoy kidding around with Ellie Mae and Ed. They kept the Babes entertained with wild stories about the years they'd worked together in Hollywood.

The tales required much body language, with Ellie Mae bouncing in Eva's salon chair and Ed twirling around in Josette's. Without Josette to help corral Ellie Mae, Eva would have had a mess on her hands.

Halfway through the coloring process, the octogenarians decided to teach the group some bawdy songs. They knew a lot of them. The more champagne they consumed, the more risque the songs. Eva hadn't laughed so hard in years. Maybe ever.

They were in the middle of *Do They Hang Too Low* when Ben Malone showed up with food from the Moose. Ellie Mae and Ed kept singing the raunchy lyrics as Henri cleared a path so he could push the multi-tiered trolley into the salon. He grinned, tipped his hat and took off, moving fast. Henri laughed and hurried after him.

Ed stopped singing. "Go get him, Henri!"

Ellie Mae and the Babes picked up their cue, chanting *get him, Henri!* until Pam waved her arms. "That's enough. They're too far down the block to hear us."

"Are they kissing?" Ellie Mae, her hair covered with strips of folded tinfoil, popped up from Eva's chair and hurried to the door, vinyl cape flapping. "I want a visual to take home with me."

Eva looked over at Josette and smiled. "She's not very good at sitting quietly, is she?"

"At least no one's suggested dancing, or I'll bet she'd be doing that. C'mon, let's go see what's happening."

"Oh, *darn*." Ellie Mae's voice carried as she moved from the doorway to the sidewalk where the others were gathered. "They're just *talking*."

"Talking's good." Peggy rose on her tiptoes to peer over Ellie Mae's thicket of foil. "Does anybody know what went on during their date Sunday night?"

"I'm convinced she's told nobody," Lucy said.

"I'd call that promising if it was special enough to keep private." Josette pulled her phone from her pocket. "Ellie Mae, it's time to check your color."

"I'll be there in a flash." She edged over to the curb so she could see down the block. "Shoot, Henri's coming back... no, wait! He grabbed her arm. He's pulling her close, aaaannnd...we have lip-lock!"

Eva's heart squeezed. Good for them. A cheer went up from the group on the sidewalk.

Ed started making shooing motions. "Okay, everyone back inside. Let them finish their kiss in peace."

"We don't all fit inside, Edna Jane."

"As many as are comfortable, then. Who wants more champagne? I'm not taking any back home."

Ellie Mae scooted back to Eva's chair. "I want more, but first I have to get my color checked."

Eva took one side and Josette the other as they each unfolded one strip of foil. "Looks great," Eva said.

Josette nodded. "Terrific. You do good work."

"Am I blue?" Ellie Mae wriggled with excitement.

"You sure are," Josette said. "Time to get you shampooed and gorgeous."

"Edna Jane, can we all go to the Moose when I'm finished so I can show it off?"

"Don't see why not. We might have to head down there, anyway, to fetch Henri."

"I love this plan. We can finish off the champagne while I'm getting beautiful and then zip down to the Moose, check on Henri and Ben, and dance a bit."

"You'll be the belle of the ball with this hair, Ellie Mae." Eva lowered the back of the chair and slipped a folded towel between Ellie's neck and the lip of the shampoo bowl. With Josette working on one side and Eva on the other, they divested her of the foil in no time.

Josette rinsed her hands. "She's all yours for the shampoo and blow dry. I'm going to treat myself to some of Ed's champagne."

"By all means. Thanks for the help."

"It was fun."

"You're a hard worker, Eva," Ellie Mae said. "I appreciate all the time you've put in."

"It's a treat doing this for you."

"Everyone's champagned up except you, Eva." Ed reclaimed Josette's chair. "Can I pour you a glass?"

"Thank you, but I'd better not. I can have cider when we go to the Moose, though." She ran warm water over Ellie Mae's hair.

"That'll be on me." Ed spun the chair. "What a great few days this has been. I can't decide which thrills me more, all the money we raised with that auction or Henri and Ben finally getting it on."

Ellie Mae closed her eyes and sighed happily as Eva worked shampoo into her hair. "Strictly speaking, Edna Jane, we don't know they're getting it on. Only that they're to the kissing stage."

"If they haven't been horizontal yet, they will be soon. Ben's not going to let grass grow under his feet. He got exactly what he wanted out of this bachelor auction."

"I'll bet he's not the only bachelor who's happy with the outcome. That cute Nick Le Grande looked overjoyed to be taking you home Sunday night, Eva."

She gulped. "Uh-huh."

"He's a strong-looking man, that's for sure. Has he completed his twelve hours of manual labor, yet?"

"Um, more or less." Her heart rate spiked. Technically he hadn't given her twelve hours, but that didn't matter anymore.

"Well, I hope it turned out well for you two. Like I said, he looked smitten on Sunday night."

"Now that you mention it, he did." Ed turned so the chair was facing Eva. "As Nick's honorary auntie, I'll put in a good word for him. He's a sweetie."

Eva took a steadying breath and concentrated on rinsing the shampoo out of Ellie Mae's hair. "Yes, he is."

"Reminds me of my first husband."

Eva glanced at her in shock. "Your *first* husband? You've had more than one?"

"Three."

"I've had four," Ellie Mae said. "I win."

"We're not done yet, Ellie Mae." She gave Eva a smile. "You never know what tomorrow will bring, right?"

"Right." Ed had been married *three times*? Ellie Mae, *four*?

Ed gazed at her. "You look quite taken aback. I admit three is a lot of husbands, but it's not in Elizabeth Taylor territory."

"No, I just... for some reason I thought you'd been single all your life like my Aunt Sally."

"She never married?"

"Never wanted to."

"Boy, I did. I adored being married to my first love, who unfortunately died in his thirties."

"That's so sad!"

"It was, and instead of letting myself grieve, I rushed into the next one. I wasn't picky about number three, either. I had to ditch him, too. Whoever ends up with Nick won't be ditching him, though. He's a keeper."

"I'm sure he is." She squeezed the water out of Ellie Mae's hair and wrapped a towel around her head. "As for me, I've decided against getting married. I'm like my aunt. I prefer my independence."

"Independence is good," Ellie Mae said. "I've always maintained mine, whether I'm married or not."

"Same here." Ed nodded. "Establishing your independence has nothing to do with being married."

"That's the truth," Ellie Mae said. "Stay away from the mean ones and the know-it-alls. Maintain your earning power. Take the kind and considerate ones like Nick. Be your own independent self, and you'll be fine."

It sounded so simple. It wasn't. Not for her.

33

Nick wasn't a designated driver and hard apple cider was working for him tonight. Just because he'd figured out why Eva was so frightened about getting married and having kids didn't mean he had answers.

In the Brotherhood's opinion, he needed to simply convince Eva she could never be a negligent parent. Not workable. Sure as the world, she'd dig in her heels if he tried that. But he had no other ideas. The cider took the edge off his frustration, so he indulged.

When the band played tunes for couples, only Leo and Garrett sought out partners. Nick stayed in the booth with the other guys and watched Henri and Ben slow dancing like newlyweds.

"It's weird," Matt said, "but in a nice way."

"She used to dance like that with Charley." Jake sipped his drink.

"Yeah." CJ exhaled. "That's the weird part. But you know what? Charley would have wanted her to find someone. He'd be cool with this."

"He liked Ben," Rafe said. "If he could have picked someone for Henri, it would be Ben."

Nick polished off his fifth bottle of cider. "Think they'll get married?" Marriage. His topic de jour.

"Don't know." Rafe gazed out at the dance floor. "But if they do, it'll be a helluva party."

The slow tune ended and the band announced *Boot Scootin' Boogie.*

Nick glanced at his brothers. "Let's do this."

"Hell, yeah, let's do this." Matt put down his bottle. "We'll bust some Brotherhood moves."

They grabbed Leo and Garrett, lined up together and proceeded to show off. Nick threw himself into it. Dancing drunk was fun. Hadn't done it in a while. He was loose. And he had this number down cold.

The message was passed along from Matt's end—*Babes in the house.* Henri was already here, but the others must have arrived. Whenever the Babes showed up at the Moose, the Brotherhood swung into action, but that didn't mean dropping out of a line dance. Nick kept going, adding flourishes whenever possible.

A flash of blue hair made him miss a step. Wait. That wasn't Eva. The blue-hair lady was with Ed and Josette. Whoops. Another blue-hair sighting. That *was* Eva. What the hell?

He stumbled, turned the wrong way and was solely responsible for a major pileup in front of her. Wonderful.

She stood at the edge of the dance floor staring at him. What was she doing here? She hardly ever came to the Moose. Why now?

He needed to get his act together. Come up with a game plan. But the Babes were here, too, which meant he had a responsibility to—

A hand gripped his shoulder. "We've got this," Rafe said. "Go talk to your lady."

He nodded and walked over to Eva. "Hi." Brilliant.

"I didn't expect to see you here."

"Ditto." More brilliance.

"I came with the Babes. Ellie Mae wanted blue hair."

"That was Ellie Mae?"

"Blue hair really changes a person."

"On the outside. Not the inside. Speaking of outside, let's go there."

She peered at him. "You're drunk."

"Pretty much."

"I've never seen you like this."

"Well, here I am. Drunk. Can we go outside?" That fifth cider was kicking in.

"Yes. I think you could use the fresh air." She took him by the arm and guided him through the front door.

He shouldn't let her do that. He should be taking her arm. That was the gentlemanly thing. Too late. They were standing on the sidewalk.

She still had a hold on his arm. "Breathe, Nick. Get oxygen into your system."

"Okay." He took several deep breaths to please her.

"Better?"

"Actually, I feel a little light-headed."

"Let's go sit on the curb."

"All right." He let her take him over to a spot where nobody was parked. He managed to sit on the curb without falling over.

"How's that?" She put a hand on his knee.

"Good. Listen, when I'm drunk, stuff just comes out of my mouth."

"You're going to throw up?"

"No, *words* come out. All kinds of words. No telling what I might say."

She smiled. "Fiona's like that, too."

"Fiona wasn't turned on by my sweat."

"What?"

"On Sunday, when you were naked and I went downstairs. She wasn't turned on."

"Were you disappointed?"

"I was *relieved.* I don't want anybody turned on but you."

"Oh."

"I made you smile again. I like it when you do that."

"I like it when you smile, too." Her voice was soft. "Nick, I'm sorry we can't... that I'm not the right..."

"*That's* what I wanted to say. They were terrible."

"Who?"

"Your folks."

"Water over the bridge."

"It's not. You remember."

She went very still. When she said something, her voice was tiny. "I do."

He wrapped his arm around her shoulders. "I remember stuff, too."

Her grip on his knee tightened. "I'm sorry."

"And I'll *never* do that to my kids."

"How do you know?" Her voice trembled.

"I just know. And you won't either. I know you, Eva. I *know you.*"

She pressed against his side. "What if you're wrong?"

"I'm not." He swallowed. "Marry me, Eva."

She started to cry.

Turning, he gathered her into his arms and rocked her back and forth. "Marry me. You know you want to."

"I do! But I'm so scared!"

"It'll get easier. I promise it will."

"You're drunk. How can I believe you?"

He tipped her wet face up to his. "I tell the truth when I'm drunk."

"You said words just come out."

"From my heart."

"Oh." She sniffed. "That's... touching."

He gazed into her green eyes, shimmering with tears. "I love you."

"I know."

"Can you love me back?"

She gulped. 'I already do. It's the scariest thing I've ever done."

"Can you say it?"

Holding his gaze, she took a shaky breath. "I love you. And I'll marry you." She squeezed her eyes shut. "I can't believe I just said that."

"I can. I danced hard. Got sweaty."

She opened her eyes and gave him a watery smile. "And I do love your sweat."

"Attagirl." He leaned down and kissed her to seal the deal. He was a little hazy about how he'd accomplished this amazing feat in the face of impossible odds, but he had her, now, and he was never, ever letting her go.

* * * * *

Cowboy Rafe Banner receives an unexpected proposal from his heart's desire, Kate Gifford, but with a catch as big as Montana in STRONG-WILLED COWBOY, book five in the Buckskin Brotherhood series!

* * * * *

*New York Times bestselling author Vicki Lewis
Thompson's love affair with cowboys started with
the Lone Ranger, continued through Maverick, and
took a turn south of the border with Zorro. She
views cowboys as the Western version of knights in
shining armor, rugged men who value honor,
honesty and hard work. Fortunately for her, she
lives in the Arizona desert, where broad-shouldered,
lean-hipped cowboys abound. Blessed with such an
abundance of inspiration, she only hopes that she
can do them justice.*

*For more information about this prolific author,
visit her website and sign up for her newsletter. She
loves connecting with readers.*

VickiLewisThompson.com

CPSIA information can be obtained
at www.ICGtesting.com
Printed in the USA
BVHW031333170820
586609BV00001B/162